Vagadu

*V*AGADU

The Adventure of Catherine Crachat: II

PIERRE JEAN JOUVE

TRANSLATED BY LYDIA DAVIS

TMP

THE MARLBORO PRESS/NORTHWESTERN

EVANSTON, ILLINOIS

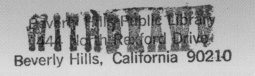

The Marlboro Press/Northwestern
Northwestern University Press
Evanston, Illinois 60208-4210

Originally published in French in 1930. Copyright © 1963 by Mercure de
France. English translation copyright © 1997 by Lydia Davis. Published 1997 by
The Marlboro Press/Northwestern. All rights reserved.

The publication of this work has been made possible in part by a grant from the
National Endowment for the Arts. The costs of translation have been met in
part by a subvention from the French Ministry of Culture.

Printed in the United States of America

ISBN 0-8101-6040-4

Library of Congress Cataloging-in-Publication Data

Jouve, Pierre Jean, 1887–
  [Vagadu. English]
  Vagadu / Pierre Jean Jouve ; translated by Lydia Davis.
      p. cm. — (The adventure of Catherine Crachat ; 2)
  ISBN 0-8101-6040-4
  I. Davis, Lydia. II. Title. III. Series: Jouve, Pierre Jean, 1887–
  Adventure of Catherine Crachat ; 2.
PQ2619.O78V313 1997
843'.912—dc21
                                                          97-18102
                                                          CIP

The paper used in this publication meets the minimum requirements of the
American National Standard for Information Sciences—Permanence of Paper
for Printed Library Materials, ANSI Z39.48-1984.

Vagadu is the force that lives in the heart of men . . .

AFRICAN LEGEND

Contents

THE ACCUSATION

I

She had come to it by degrees. After all those hesitations, those
tentative moves, after many periods of agitation in public and at
home, and all those repeated nights of anguish that spilled over
into her life and made the day impossible, after the fits of uneasiness, blockage, paralysis, the pointless and resourceless new begin-
nings, she had experienced sudden intense chills, an uncontrol-
lable urge to vomit, and a state of melancholy, her head in her
skirts; so that she at last found herself in the unfamiliar room of
this man, lying down, at his disposition. He behind her and she
before him. He was sitting in a leather armchair. Catherine was
going to understand the Thing that lies behind; for in life there is
always an essential thing behind one. As real as this man in his
armchair, silent. "I am going to learn what has always been, my
secret, me. He will have to tell it to me." For this thing has always
been there in order to impel and impede one's actions; it is the
Past, it is also the present; and now, said this lady, this thing must
be dead and decayed. It still stops me from living as I should,
even today. We'll see, all right.

   She thought about when she was a little girl. Someone named
Bob was always pulling at her skirt, but he was doing it to find
out what was underneath. "Is that man in the armchair going to
look at my underwear, too?" Madame C. gave an odd smile at
this idea and felt her heart thumping inside her, like the heart of
a bird that has just been caught. Turning around was not allowed.
"If you turn around, you will change into a pillar of salt, like
Lot's wife." Monsieur Leuven is Jewish anyway. He is not beautiful. His red lips are very noticeable in his beard. Looking at it,
one sensed something thick, mysterious, imperfectly covered
over by the innocent color. "He never says anything. Maybe he

doesn't know how to talk?" His ears are pointed like the ears of mythological creatures, his curly fleece is already scanty; in a flowered vest, this fine gentleman of forty years displays his belly, and his clothes, of a fine material, have become baggy through improper use. "I'm sure that he has his hands, his plump hands, lying flat on his thighs."

And Madame C. repeated to herself the Negro's consoling prayer: "*God is behind me—I am behind Him—God is before me—I am with Him.*" Then M. Leuven explained the rules of the game, which could be summed up thus: you will say exactly what comes into your mind. Madame C. agreed to this. Catherine's eyes scanned the room. Lord, it was ugly! Before she came, since one has to form an idea, the lady had decided that the decor would be Louis XVI and Gobelins, quite uninteresting. But look at this! She found herself in a large room painted in a shiny enamel the color of prune juice; the carpets were rubber and the heavy hangings above were silk. His desk was amazing, of steamship-style teakwood, with an enormous plaster sculpture. But where does this room get its light from? No windows can be seen. From what direction? He occupies a large number of rooms in this wealthy neighborhood where he lives, but if the avenue is like this, the street like that, then the carriage entrance, the staircase having two directions, the waiting room, and lastly this room, how did it happen that the room was facing the way she felt it was? "No, we're not looking out toward the Opéra. Are we looking toward the square?" "I don't understand how the room can have this shape and at the same time look out toward the square." The visitor decided to start her examination, her analysis, over again. There was nothing else to do. It was agreed that she would speak when she wanted to; silence has to be paid for here; silence is golden. But it was not useful to tell him that his furniture was perfectly suited to Jews in the export business and diamond merchants, gaudy and conventional—in a word, conventional. Let's start over, she said to herself, and orient the house. A feeling of distress warned her that she wouldn't manage to do it; the neighborhood took on many different shapes, depending on what side one approached it from; the house and the room in the house could be positioned in any direction. "I'm starting from the avenue. The avenue runs off at an angle in relation to the Seine, but wait, sorry, I'm wrong, it's the Seine that bends. Not well thought out at all. Let's start from the Arc de Triomphe, no, from the Colonne. The north and the south. But if the north . . . " Fortunately, no one heard her say the most vulgar word to herself. "And why the devil am I here? I don't need to be here with this German at all." But she noticed that she was not getting up from her place to leave, on the contrary, she was settling in. In the avenue, which ran from the southwest to the northeast, she had passed close to a little garden; one could see a little garden there. "My little garden. Little Garden Street. It is very, very far away; he kissed me chastely with a touch of his lips in Little Garden Street." By distorting M. Leuven, one got Leuve, Leuvre, *lèvres*—lips. "Monsieur Leuvre," she thought, "has legs like stovepipes"; and she felt that she would soon come to hate him. Enough! She would have either to leave it or enter it, this diabolical room, but at all costs break the silence, which horrified her. She noticed that she was twisting her hands.

Lèvre or Leuvre had to be looking at her as she lay there; for she was one of those women who matter, when they are lying down. "Lying down, I present a spectacle that is not unpleasant." Certainly Leuvre would not be losing a single detail; besides, he wore glasses. How was she to get him to talk, and how was she to figure out how the room was oriented? "If I head down the hallway from left to right . . . and the windows . . . from right to left . . . Those windows are not street windows, because listen to the silence here: like cotton wool, it smothers shouts, absorbs tears. And what if I go back to the waiting room again as though I were leaving? By taking . . . at the entrance . . . *Basta, mia cara.* No more hope for you." She was extremely disturbed, she was wounded by the fact that she had not been able to orient the room properly. She said, "It's too much" and "I'm a clod," and she turned so that her other hip lay on the bed. At that moment Leuv. asked her what she was thinking. She answered that she was thinking he had an unpleasant voice and that his furniture was vulgar.

"But what annoys me the most is that I can't figure out whether this room faces the theater or the public garden."

"Why do you need to know that?" asked M. Leuven. She said nothing in reply. "You haven't got it. The room faces the factory chimney you saw when you came in."

"Oh." Catherine was truly vexed, but this Leuv. was right.

DEMOLITION EQUIPMENT

Catherine returned home and was very surprised to find her dressing room in a state of upheaval. This furnished dressing room has a more or less classical, rococo style, because a part of Madame C.'s life, and some memories, are attached to Vienna. It was not just that the dressing room was disorderly—the effect of objects lying around, as happens when there are stockings on the floor and a sponge on the piano! The signification of the dressing room had changed.

Catherine, stricken, hardly recognized the place, her place. Everything had been shifted on the walls, the furniture was misshapen. Surely the wallpaper had been redone while she was away. The effect was *different.* She never used objects like these. Prints had been put up on the paneling, for instance, one close to the next: they touched. Prints? Postcards, stuck up with thumbtacks. These were the subjects depicted: the lake, painted blue; a pretty stream in autumn; smoke wisps up from a little cottage with a thatched roof in the evening; a fat robin goes chirp, chirp, and chirp in the briar patch; children whose clothes are made of real, clinging satin throw snowballs at each other! And so on. All this in very bad taste. Once again, frightful, "cheap," and in frightfully bad taste.

Catherine received the answer to the mystery when she saw her friend Flore. The latter had assumed an English identity. Arrogant, she wore a flared dress, too long in the back (at least in Catherine's opinion) but in the Victorian mode, with all sorts of frills and furbelows, laces and pendants hanging below her waist. "This," thought Catherine, "must be why she ordered a pair of high-quality silk underpants for four hundred francs." She contented herself with saying to Flore: "Good evening, dear. How very décolleté you are!"

But the other said, "I know what I'm doing." She pointed to the postcards. "My brother from London gave them to me. Anyway, I adore England!" No need to say how these peculiar words, branded with spite, capable of turning your blood by the venom of jealousy they secreted, touched Catherine's heart.

Catherine had a horror of vulgar displays, even more than of usurpations and changes imposed on her dressing room.

"Trimegiste is coming," added Flore, "to show off his remarkable outfit."

And in fact Trimegiste appeared. Could Flore possibly—dismal supposition—have a feeling of love for Trimegiste? Anyway, this Trimegiste had become a painter and enjoyed the same fame as Flore, who had become a great lady.

"What do you think of my outfit?" remarked M. Trimegiste after kissing the hands of the two friends. He was dressed as a modern Hamlet. That is, he wore a rather tight-fitting smoking jacket, one of his legs in a black pant leg, and the other in a pink silk tight from his belt to his pump.

M. Trimegiste bowed deeply to Flore, advancing the foot that belonged to the pink leg.

"Let's leave them!" cried Catherine, and she went out quickly. From this moment on, she was not very sure of the time or the place. Was the reality of her life changing its nature to such an extent? She was in a sad-looking room. Then another room, empty. A succession of rooms. Maybe Catherine had landed somehow on the story below? Ever since leaving Leuv.'s, she had felt really too tired. But a wind was driving her from one room to the next, and from a known ill to another even more indistinct. Driven across, at last, into a dark recess, she *fell* there upon an unfamiliar couch.

She was holding P. in her arms. Who? What P.? Pierre. The man she had loved, whom she talked about so often to Trimegiste, and who had died. About fifty centimeters long. He was made of wood or some other material and dressed as Francis of Assisi. It was that the *poverello* died without having done anything. C. C. was delighted to have found him again at last and wanted to sleep with him, when . . . a window they had not seen opened on the lovers! The window opened noisily. A window filled with the din, clamor, etc., of a crowd on the boulevard. All the intersecting and mingled words of the crowd had a meaning, and as soon as one heard the sound, one recognized the meaning; it was something like: "Drive them away! Kick them out! Get rid of them!" or maybe "Drive them out! Drive them out! Drive them out!" The voice of the crowd was not so clear, but the flood of its words broke the dike of the window with a terrible, irresistible malice: putting the idea into execution, it threatened the two unfortunates with death. Not a minute to lose! Catherine recovered the confidence of her movements. No more fits of weakness! She took him by the hand, he was now of normal size. "Let's get out of here! Come." And they ran off.

. . . .

Or rather, it was he who had taken her by the hand. They ran through the mountains and forests for a very long time. They were going off together, though they didn't know where, for when you are being hunted together, you don't need to know where. There they were now, in some beautiful meadows. Everything that grew in them had the color of youth. Thus they arrived at dusk in a delicious small valley. The days were greatly lengthened that day. They did not fail to remark that "the air was mild for the season." A small stream flowed down the middle, deeply embanked under the brambles. How very beautiful and pretty it seemed! And melancholy! All in all, how pleasing it was. Glug-glug . . . glug-glug . . .

He said:

Here, two streams hidden 'neath bridges of green . . .

She answered:

Pass caressing the curves of the valley . . .

While her foot, alas too lightly shod, sank into the black mold. And He, during that time, touching with a bold finger her waist and sometimes her young breast, guided her across, and into the dark bower, on the road full of obstacles.

And it was now that they saw the Hunter!

Hee, hee! Now wasn't he fine-looking. Handsome as the pope and green as moss. And a double-barreled gun. His gray-black dog, neither black nor gray, followed at his heels, because a dog is supposed to follow his master. She did not like the fierce dog— no, she didn't like him—but on the other hand she admired the way the tall hunter was covered in leather, for the huntsman's sacred calling. And his beard with its red mouth, of the same color as the leather. Meanwhile, the Hunter, controlling his wild dog, looked askance at them, at her and her young consort.

In the distance a village appeared. In this picture-book country the colors were painted, and against the green of the forests they had painted the gray of an old village. Now it was Pierre say-

9

ing "I'm off," and (small again) he entered the street where the brothels were and disappeared into a house. Abandoned, she was alone. Alone? No, with the Hunter. The Hunter was larger than any other object. He hid the entire landscape.

The Hunter set the dog with the gray-black coat upon Catherine. Catherine was so afraid that she wet her bottom, but still, he was good-looking, that Hunter, and she ran, and she ran, and she really hoped the filthy dog wouldn't be able to get her! But she was so afraid that in the village square, where she arrived panting, she saw a pyre of wood, and was certain it was for her. Faggots, trees, sticks! It rose to the height of the rooftops. And Catherine was so afraid she rushed up onto it, shouting, "I must, I must, I must!" and really understood what this wood had been gathered for, for Catherine's pyre, and the dog was still trying to get hold of her hand, but the dog did not succeed, given that on Catherine's finger there was a metal ring.

The people were still bringing sticks, on and on. She suffered what one suffers when one is burning. "I have to see just a little more." She wanted to go on "seeing." That was her last thought. On one side she was burning, and on the other she was prolonging her life because she insisted on seeing.

"Wouldn't you rather pass out?"

In the end she agreed. "Yes, I'd rather pass out."

This was the end of the horrible journey.

* * *

Catherine woke up at the usual time, in her bed, and she was still overwhelmed by sleep as she was already rapidly reviewing her most important memories, her most important feelings, and concluding: it is natural to live. Catherine's mind, when she awakens, goes much faster than her body. Thus she discovered later that one of her legs was folded in a V on top of the other and her back was tired, aching, and her bedclothes had formed little rumples under her.

She had thought, before feeling that leg and that back, of a story; she had forgotten it right away. "Once, in another house in my life, I was wakened by the concert of birds at every season. Then it was wonderful to wake up!" "My eyes weren't so rheumy and my bottom so heavy in those days." In this way she avoided thinking of something less pleasant, which was still in the background. She noticed that her mind was completely clear, but her body motionless and her eyes carefully closed. "It would be very easy, if one knew how, to suppress the tiresome daily part of one's life; one would think about anything one wanted and one would look like a statue. It's when I open my eyes again that my anguish returns and I feel I am a martyr."

She looked at the half-dark room, and it seemed to her she had dreamed a great deal. "I dreamed of complicated things." She told herself, on the other hand, that Paris on a foggy day was completely familiar to her. Unfortunately, she would be too sad to enjoy it. The streets are straight and pink; in them one sees an aged poverty. The sun is barely visible and the smell is that of locomotive smoke. But she took up her thought again: that she had dreamed a great deal. She had dreamed of a fancy costume and . . . of bathing in a stream. Then she corrected it: "I dreamed of Shakespeare first, and then of a dog." She thought, believing she had dreamed about two things, that one does not necessarily dream in twos, but in threes, fours, and even more. And what one remembers is not what one has dreamed.

She eased her discomfort by moving. She turned on the light switch and took a book from the shelf. It was, in fact, the book of "her Saint." She read at random in the book. It was, in fact, the story of the Lord replacing the Saint's heart with his own shining, red heart. She turned the pages in bunches. It was the story of the afflictions: "*Io ho eletto le pene per mio refrigerio . . .*" Seeing that the Saint had chosen her afflictions, Catherine called out to Flore with all her strength.

Flore came quickly to open the shutters. The sun entered. There is nothing like the sun to deliver us from the night. "And if the love of the Saint would deliver us from life, that would be even better." Flore was a gentle, reasonable creature who looked as though she were made of wallpaper. Her conventional presence reassured you right away. However, she looked a little puffy this morning; she had just come back from Les Halles. "I went to Les Halles for you," she specified, and made her entrance again, carrying in her arms an enormous bunch of roses, for Flore, as her name indicates, adores flowers, and what she likes is to go and find them in the market itself, at daybreak, not far from the meat sections. She explained how she had chosen the colors: garnet and white, and more garnet than white; the garnet was quite special, the white exceptional. After that, Flore remains a little puffy until noon.

While Catherine had lunch, she did not talk about Monsieur Leuven, whom she had been to see, nor of what went on there. "I will have to tell Flore about it," she thought. But she remained silent. Thus another life detached itself from her ordinary life, since she did not talk about it to Flore. She burned to go back there.

* * *

"Good day, Madame!"

Pointless for you to bow that way, she sighed. "Good day, Monsieur."

"Good day, Madame!" So he was not able to say anything else but these cunning phrases? And was this all he had in the way of social amenities? Oh, of course! He wanted to contribute his share, but it was quite ridiculous. In his sumptuous apartment, adjoining the waiting room, there was a closet, and it was here that he received her! Oh, of course! A hole with no space and no other way out, unlit, and next door to the bathrooms. In there one was disgusted to the point of thinking nasty thoughts. But the bearing she maintained was of the most fashionable order. Yet M. Leuven did not appear to suspect . . . and kept bowing. Catherine made a tour of the walls. Nothing on one and nothing on the other; pretty tale of wretchedness; and now, once again, she entered into an extreme distress. "How ugly it all is, and what is going to happen to me?" She was accompanied by Leuven and some other people. "What is going to happen to me?" It was pointless to look at those others, to try to find out their names. She had been familiar with them for a long time. They were: them. From those, such as they were, there was no mercy to be hoped for.

However, in those walls the unhappy woman saw a corridor open up. She followed it to the end. Now imagine a wide terrace covered with grass. From here one could look out over the whole city. The orientation was easy. There was a May sky over this city (for the beginning of our story takes place in May), lofty and magnificent, of the purest splendor. Off to the side certain small hills had been planted with vines. But she had seen this sight many, many times.

Where?

The spectacle was composed, in this magnificent setting, among the vine leaves, of lots and lots of small personages dressed, my God, in velvet and coarse muslin, as in the old days, or like charming dolls in the fashion of the day: the men feminine with graceful pants, and the women flat, nice-looking, in their manly outfits. Farther off, tall trees grew in the French style. They all seemed very cheerful and very young, and the mere sight of them gave pleasure.

They were agreeable, they were tender. How prettily they moved, these little human butterflies. Because they had been overlaid with the famous brilliant colors. And the city was in fact full of thousands of sparkling mirrors that were windows transformed so as to reflect on every side the crowd of characters. Catherine was at last happy, watching these little people, the sky, the trees, and many neighborhoods and neighborhoods of houses that belonged to her. And the hill, and all those handsome vineyards, and all the little vineyard people. And the costumes, and the crowd of little men, and the sky, and the large sky, and all the things of Catherine's, of Catherine's imagination and love.

* * *

Monsieur Leuv. turned around in his chair. Several people must have smoked cigars in this room before Catherine arrived, for the air smelled like a toilet. When Catherine returned home, she swore to herself: "Today I'm talking to Flore about it." Yet she did not talk that day, or the next. A Sunday followed, she did not go to Leuven's, but still she did not talk about it. "Well," Catherine said to herself, "the fact is I shouldn't be talking about it, and in fact what is inside me is already so changed, it would be senseless to talk about it." The tea that Flore had bought at Kirdomah's especially for Catherine was simply delicious and that was the main thing. Then Catherine had her third adventure, which was this:

She was walking on a road that went uphill. The slope was very steep. The road rose so abruptly that as one walked up, one felt one's feet were made of lead. This was in the country near the Alps, and you know the landscape. On the road a cart full of dung climbed slowly on a calm summer morning.

That morning, on the road, there were Catherine and the cart. No one else. On the front of the cart stood the carter. The tall carter, standing in the cart, was looking straight ahead of him.

Why was he looking ahead? Because he was furious. Why did this tall carter seem furious? Because, you see, he had his back turned to his horse. And so who was he looking at? Catherine.

No one as far as the eye could see.

Poor Catherine was therefore obliged to walk behind this dung cart in order to try to catch up with it. She had to exert herself on the upgrade, as they say. Meanwhile, the furious carter kept his eye on her, as they say, and shouted two words at her: "Come here!" The carter was saying: "Come here," "God Almighty," and "Get your ass closer!" and other curses even more vulgar, which a woman now grown up like the real Catherine would not be able to bear listening to. He was saying, "Bloody whore," and "Get your shitty self on up here," and other more horrible things, and always ended with "Closer!" The carter was holding a shovel. The shovel was loaded with manure. The carter jiggled the shovel, and manure fell on Catherine.

The carter was red with anger. He was shouting "Come closer!" and Catherine came as close as she could, as close as she could on such a difficult road. The carter loaded his shovel and Catherine came even closer, the carter jiggled the shovel, manure flew through the air before falling on Catherine, and Catherine was covered with filth.

He was red with anger.

Abreast of her came Pierre, or the man she loved. He was as small, as wretched as she, and soon he was covered with manure like her. Then she explained to him, pointing to the powerful carter: "You see him. Well, that's your father." But he protested, since the carter was certainly not his father. She replied: "Yes, he is your father, *the one who came before you.*" Pierre persisted in saying no. (The fool, he should have understood: the one who came before you—the one who had me before you.)

II

These material components of her thought, when examined in the light of day, were like so many enigmas. Yet one was struck by the force of what they were trying to say. Catherine, already dazed, saw that the moment was coming when she would have to be courageous. She noticed a long rope. She took a strong grip on it. Then she felt she was in empty space. She let herself slide, and plunged downward.

HOLE

"Let us imagine an earth that moves, that sinks; that becomes hollow as it sinks, that loosens, that softens and at last disappears inside, into a gulf; this earth, as it flows, takes the form of a vast sinkhole. I am on this earth, I am going down with it, in the same motion. On the sides, stones, detached pieces, small bits of gravel come sliding down, making a melancholy noise that irresistibly evokes the word: irreparable. But—this is not a simple sinkhole, nor is it a burrow, rather it is a piece of machinery impelled by a gyratory motion. For the sides are turning, and the motion, accelerating as I descend farther, draws me irresistibly farther below the surface.

"Unable to hold myself back with anything, I look down toward the bottom. On the bottom I see two animals that are fighting, not fighting, two animals, not absolutely two animals, not fighting but rolling around and struggling, not two animals but two people. I see them in profile or full-face according to the gyratory motion of the machinery, for it turns and changes ceaselessly, and it keeps on falling into the depths of some place. I recognize one of these people by her bosom, it's me. The other I don't know. But I shall willingly name him: the stranger. The first of these people is therefore a woman adorned with a bosom, who suffers what I suffer; the second will be known much later, unless he is the emanation of this German doctor, Loew., sitting in an armchair and occupied with listening, unless it is a leopard or some other superb beast that I will be able to appropriate some day. The simplest thing would be to call him: Stranger. He answers to that name: look at him blink his eyes. But let's admit that everything is true *together* and I must superimpose many figures, many impressions, to give you an idea of the creature that is assaulting me. This is why we are fighting, biting each other, and blood is flowing abundantly."

* * *

"Hole, depth. One digs. One decends into the interior. One sees into oneself. So one is therefore at home, in one's heart, and it is warm there, do you understand me? Hole, sinkhole, cone in the earth, means to go deep into one's flesh, exploring. The noise of stones falling along the sides signifies that never again will this be the flat earth, the easy life of former times.

"'I love you.'

"Why did I say that? For I do not love you. You are the object of what I feel. What I feel is infinitely strong and would not exist without you. Because my emotion needs to be deposited. I am depositing it on *you*.

"I feel the ardor, the heat of affection, and naturally I think of you. This warmth, this fever . . . it's very good. You are new in my life, and you are ferreting out my secrets. The heat, the ardor are for you. Nothing could be more natural.

"You are strong, you are sensual; I sense you very well, despite the fact that you are hidden behind me; it is pleasant to feel you through your masculine smell. Your voice reassures me. A man's beauty lies in his charm rather than his features. And why the animals in a hole? They are biting each other, they are bleeding. No doubt because I am suffering, and no doubt because of the struggle I have to endure. A horror has begun; it's a battle against you and with you, and you have to give me your help.

"While I am talking to you, I feel physical sensations that are apparently caused by your hand. If I say your hand . . . I mean the idea of your hand; because I know that you are very correct. At the same time I feel them exactly as though you were doing it. I put together the sensation and the knowledge I have that it is not real: this produces a very curious effect. Nevertheless, the pleasure and the fear are such that I would not be able to detach myself from it; it no longer has to exist.

"This thing was making me feel ashamed, but now that I've told you about it, I see it isn't so interesting after all and I sense in myself a desire to laugh at it. Why should I take everything I tell you seriously? Again, the false trying to pass for the true!"

* * *

After talking this way, Catherine looked for a place to be alone. She wanted a room and walls, and that no living creature would enter there; but such solitude is difficult to preserve in a large city. It's better to enter the crowd, where one is just as alone for as long as necessary. She often haunted the metro and the streets in the center of town, those crowded spots where objects and people mingle. In this solitude, the various parts of her life looked at her and asked her questions. For instance, her birth, daughter of a father studying medicine at Vachette and of a mother who was a mistress he had married; first they lived in the rue Monge; then in the country. She was on the farm because her father had taken over the practice of a country doctor (he wore his hat on the back of his head and smoked one pipe after another), but also because they wanted to protect her from the disease they all had; in fact, her two sisters, her father, her mother, all soon died within the space of two years. Catherine, in the midst of the packed streets, tried to discover with regard to these memories: is this important or not? At the same time she thirsted for silence, but she found herself surrounded by an uproar.

It was very true that she had not married; she had had a childhood in little rural backwaters, nothing but bad memories, and a youth in the gutter. It was true that she had never done anything seriously: "neither wife, nor artist, nor prostitute, but a little of each." It was true that she had had a lover, halfway, and had lost him because he died. She felt her age, every bit of her age.

* * *

Soon Catherine oriented herself differently with relation to M. Leuven, following the small event we are going to recount. She was with him. Suddenly a great whirlwind arrives and develops, wraps around her, along with the apartment, with the things and the entire space. This falling motion, as she turned around and around, made Catherine lose consciousness, and she came out of it, much later, it seemed to her, when she woke up; or rather, when she returned to life from death. She asked where she was. Her heart knocked against her chest, hurting her. The feelings were dismal; but she remembered very clearly that the movement of falling had been accompanied by an acute happiness. Her first words after the fall were: "I really would like to be loved." She was beside herself, on the other hand, to see that Monsieur Leuven had remained calmly sitting. Had he been absorbed by a momentary distraction, or by the pleasure of chewing on his dead cigar? In any case, he had allowed her to faint.

Catherine sensed that her feelings were hardening and solidifying against such a strange gentleman.

Yet she recounted how she had always cherished a certain reverie of finding herself in a very isolated room that would suddenly fly up into the air and plunge into infinity, moving from left to right. And Catherine—since to emerge from a faint is to be reborn—began to talk about the idea of her birth without rhyme or reason: "I have to confess to you that it horrifies me to be a woman. This *fons vitae* disgusts me. I never think calmly about my mother's womb. That flesh in which I am imprisoned, that water, to be part of her, to receive her blood, is intolerable to my imagination. And to be conceived! Conceived in the lowest part of her, after encountering another low thing! No. I want to reduce myself to *me*. I don't want to be sustained or fed. I don't accept tranquillity, comfort. I have refused, of course, the woman's noble role. I am a woman, that's possible. Too bad. It happened despite me. You won't make me change about that!"

III

THE THEATER BOX

When she entered the hall, went into her stage box, she looked around and was surprised that a theater as trashy as this could still exist. Really, this one went beyond all bounds. The cornices supported by caryatids with swollen breasts, the pillars decorated with angels blowing trumpets, the copious velvets, the curtain bearing a second, a third, and a fourth curtain in trompe l'oeil, and a multitude of sculpted ornaments on every level, such as panpipes, bouquets of violets, queens from decks of cards, bagpipes, and little palisades—this seemed truly unthinkable in our time. There were many people in the theater, chattering, saying hello, exchanging compliments before the hour when the curtain was to rise. Fans fluttered at the ends of bare arms; as for the men, one couldn't talk about them at first glance, they appeared rather dark. The uproar was intense.

When one goes to the Opéra, it can give one the impression of a last judgment, the people are so solemn and well dressed. But in this hall there was nothing like that. The public was a crowd of clerks, novelty salesmen, who had come with wives and children, at ease and perfectly content because they had paid for their seats. Nevertheless, Catherine settled herself comfortably for the nice little evening she was going to spend with Flore, seeing the play everyone was talking about. She retouched her hair with a finger, the curl which men prefer, she straightened her neckline, and at last sat down in her beautiful dress of sea-green silk—when, on the front of the stage, leaning back against the cardboard curtain, appeared a tall figure.

He was looking at the audience, but in truth at a different audience than this bunch of vulgar people, a more intelligent, more distinguished audience: in short, he was looking only at Catherine in her stage box.

The stage manager—for it was he—had something to say. His impersonal face suited a stage manager. His round arms and legs in his black suit were like stovepipes. When the hall saw the stage manager on the stage, it rustled, and there was a heavy silence. A door banged on an upper level, because one lady, overcome by too strong an emotion, found herself obliged to go out. The stage manager waited until silence, a sufficient silence, should be established. The silence was complete, but for the stage manager, given the importance of what he had to communicate, the silence was not yet silent enough. And until absolute silence should be created, something he had decided to have, he would keep his mouth half-open.

Catherine regretted very much having ventured into this comic theater, where scandal was going to break out; at this moment everyone's attention and interest were caught suddenly. The manager was deigning to speak. The manager said one word; that word was a name; the name . . .

That name seemed to Catherine the most ignoble utterance she had ever heard from a human mouth. The worst name that ever was. The concert hall, filled with people, full to bursting, let her know by its swelling murmur, followed by the sort of prostration one observes in funerals, that she had understood perfectly. Yet the name, which rolled thus through the hall, represented only a half of what the manager had to say, since he had only said, CATHERINE! But the manager opened his mouth for the second time, still addressing the most intellectual and best part of the audience. And when he then pronounced

. . . CRACHAT!

a horrible storm rose from all the tiers, and Catherine was on her feet in her box. Of course she knew very well that her name was not a beautiful name. But she had never thought anyone would make her feel ashamed . . . "There she is, caught in front of everyone." "Yes," she answered, reeling, "I have to go through this. But it's too, too, too humiliating!" Already the theater was emptying, and the salesmen were going home, commenting on the event.

* * *

The day after that memorable "stage box," Catherine was broken with fatigue. She was broken by a fatigue that was not natural, by a fatigue that went beyond all fatigue of whatever kind. She went out and walked a little along the quays of the river, going from one bridge to the next.

What does all this mean? It was fine, very fine, bright weather, a bright sun, though wrapped in very pleasant mists; the first swallows were crossing high up in the picture. All the colors were delicate. All the stones, pretty. The white stones. Everywhere the great city of stones. The distant lines of the capital in cut stone, and a French flag. Stone.

Pierre.

Why had he died. Why does one die. And why. Why had he loved her like that, but left her like that. Why, when she had found him again by chance in that damned country back there, was it just on the eve of his death. Why did he die right after. Why did his death occur just after he told her "I love you" for the second time. It's the second time that counts. Why hadn't he married her immediately instead of proposing that ideal to her, and other things of that kind. Why had he wanted . . . the opposite—in fact—the opposite of what should be done. And then why had he disappeared. By what right had he died. Is one permitted to disappear as though through a trapdoor? But this series of sensational events in his life seemed, just like the stone of the big city, exterior. It was because Catherine was clinging to life outside, that day, that she was going over his memory like this. The more she did it, the more she felt that the real harm was in another place; and in that place no space and no emptiness, no time and no anything else, and just one single person. It would certainly be necessary to leave on a dangerous voyage, if one ever wanted to reach it.

"I am no longer where I was," confessed Madame C., "and I am no longer the same."

It was possible to continue holding herself back. The condemned man delays his execution as long as he can, from one hour to the next. There are no smaller or more ridiculous means to preserve what we have. She had many sensations that morning next to the river's parapet. She excited herself so as to have still more, in order to stop herself from falling into "the other side," or the shadow. The green lawns were green and iridescent, not otherwise. The fast cars that received the sun in their faces gleamed like racing cars, and not otherwise. The sky was the color of periwinkle, not otherwise. At midday ordinary men, named Gontran, for instance, met ordinary women, named Prune, for instance, and made dates with them in an affected way, and not otherwise. Things experienced seemed natural and necessary. Thus a woman *like the others* was walking with lassitude on that quay. She continued on her way. She had the elegance of a beauty that is reproduced on postcards. Thus this woman stood out from the others in a certain way; if she had not had fashionable society, fashionable society had had her . . . The world is brutish, it is true. This is a city or a cloud or a society. Something definite, without danger, without equivocation, reassures us absolutely.

(Unlike the Other, the shadow, the state of being inside and no longer outside, and unlike dreaming, unlike the solely interior moment—if one belongs to "oneself" and if one abandons oneself—and unlike the appearance that results in certain objects, draperies, faces, etc., and the *language* that *this speaks*—across certain eddies or rather dispositions or perhaps formidable thickenings . . .)

Catherine, putting her hand on the stone of the parapet, scratched the stone a few times.

She noticed a little girl.

Under the chestnuts and acacias, the little girl's brown velvet created a pretty effect. The child was waving a jump rope and playing all alone. Having contrived to be alone, the child was turned inward and did not notice anything else: she did not see Catherine. But she was talking; she let furtive thoughts come out, in a quiet voice that passed between her little lips as precious as rose leaves. "A boy, a boy, a boy?" asked the little girl with the doleful air of a dream, and appearing to wake up she looked to one side to see if the world would answer her appeal. But the world did not bring her any boy. Then she said "Oh . . . " in acknowledgment of so bitter a misfortune. And yet in order to evade the misfortune, she decided to make the misfortune into a game, and to sing her misfortune—"A boy! A boy! A boy!"—in a rapid, martial tone as she turned the rope. And jumping more and more quickly, each time she crossed the rope she now shouted "A boy!" with a sort of joyful ferocity.

Catherine quivered as though the little girl's rope had whipped her on the skin, and she hurried home.

BATH SCENE

The place was entirely white and, on its shining surface, covered with eyes that rose all the way up to the ceiling, tranquil and hygienic; it was always reassuring to enter the place because of those eyes on the wall, whose gaze was white on white. Once the bolt was turned twice, one felt one was in a pure place, surrounded and tranquilized. The supply pipes ran up on the outside of the wall, rigid and white like the cube. The masses of porcelain were three in number and the whole thing of a heavy style. The faucets turned wonderfully to fill it up with transparent water. There was only one word to say. In addition, the control knobs for the jet of water in the bidet and the snake of the shower; and the drain valves, the waste pipes like basses in the orchestra; then the nickeled tubes and the glass surfaces; and on these sacred objects the silvery white of the walls, the white, with the eyelids of eyes that open gently on the wall at different heights.

In this bathroom one was in *Susanna's* position. But one was observed by a gaze that did not debase but ennobled. What was more, because of the intended purpose of the place, it was fully licit. To enter the water was not always necessary. It was enough to experience the relaxation after turning the bolt, and to put off one's veils before the enamel paint's mysterious eyes.

After the morning walk on which she had seen the little girl, Catherine came in and sat down, as usual turned the bolt, dropped her clothes, and remained there. She was very red in the face, and her staring eyes sought the eyes she had become accustomed to seeing, in her imagination, on the wall. The eyes responded very much and in great number. This caused her to look at herself with the greatest care, through the soapless water.

She inspected herself with pleasure, and as she did so she felt impelled to do it more, and she lost herself, so to speak, in what she was seeing. She also sought, as she did this, a quantity of images of herself in her memory, and smells, and forgotten gestures. At first she had simply looked at herself; soon she saw herself contemplated by the woman who was most intimate with her. "Oh pretty one! Oh adorable one!" were the words she heard, and the words came from her, from the one who was studying her, but were savored by her, the beautiful body in the bathtub.

A new, pleasant solitude came into being, for the eyes of the wall, discreetly, gave way before Catherine's own eye, they yielded to its dazzling superiority. In such a feeling of superiority one may find happiness; happiness came at its most intense, then Catherine seemed to fall asleep.

She did not know why she had often thought, in this bath, about Jesus, then about his poor body, and about Leuven, that damned imbecile whom she had begun to love. As she stood up, she probably dripped everywhere; after that the thoughts she had had in the tub came back to her, but infinitely sad and as though covered in ashes. "I'm catching cold" was how she described it to herself. And even as she expressed this idea, she noticed that she was still unclothed in a heavy state of torpor, a state "that had no limits," "whose end she could not see." Probably a long time went by. She must have made some motions too, to warm herself, and sat down again without moving. We don't know what happens, in fact, when an important and endless meditation takes over our being. And to her great stupefaction she saw Flore, in her city clothes, whereas she herself was still quite naked; she certainly could not help realizing that Flore was inside the bathroom.

"But I'd locked the door."

"What's the matter with you?" cried Flore, looking at the large forsaken body, with its heavy breasts, its right hand hanging like a claw and its left hand extending down a thigh to pick up a stocking that was falling.

She said, "I've caught cold."

Flore covered her back, her shoulders. "All the doors are open from the vestibule to here!"

"No, they were locked."

Flore stopped dressing Catherine to say, "The proof is—here I am!"

Catherine smiled, wretchedly, a great wretched smile, like a sick woman.

The sick woman.

* * *

In fact, Flore was holding a letter addressed to Catherine that had arrived by express mail. C.C., already back in her natural role, became absorbed in reading the following lines:

"Madame,

"You do not know me. You have never seen me. Yet I am writing to you in my present distress, because I know that you care for my poor papa, who before falling ill (for my papa is ill, he has typhoid fever) often spoke of you to me. Even at the beginning of his illness he advised me to write to you, and why I did not do it I have no idea; I have so many things on my hands. All of this has happened so quickly, and gone so badly. I am the daughter of M. Parchemin, who was your publicity agent, and my name is

Noémi. We were in a hotel in the rue Monsieur-le-Prince, because I must tell you we generally live in Pau, and my papa came to Paris to get treated for a chronic illness; and he also had to settle me in Paris because I am a student. My mother died last summer, and my papa has had a great deal of sorrow. Since we were alone, we came here at Christmas. He had scarcely arrived in Paris when he caught the flu. It's nothing, I said to myself, and I looked after him in our room. But he never really recovered fully, and finally, in March, he caught typhoid fever. He was taken to Saint Joseph's Hospital, but there it was difficult because my papa has no religious convictions. So with the last money I possess I had him put in a nursing home, whose address I am sending you. This is the thirty-ninth day of the typhoid fever, and his heart is affected as well as his kidneys, unfortunately. My papa is very sick. Come see him, Madame, I beg you.

"With admiration and devotion, on papa's part and mine,

"Noémi Parchemin."

IV

She was on her way to Leuven's, as always, when in the street she suddenly felt (the effect of a draft?) her left eyelid close, and remain closed. She rubbed the area of the eye with her gloved finger. In vain; her eyelid, having come down all the way over her eye, prevented her from seeing.

Having now only one eye to see with, her course, as she walked on, was a slightly crooked one. She was very upset. Upset, yes, considerably so; upset because of that eye closed by a leaden eyelid, and despite her saying to herself it will pass, it is passing, and that she was not really worried because she knew it would pass. And she remembered that once, in the rue Jacob days, when she was "very much in love," after he had left her, she had had an inflammation of the nerve in that same eye, and that when looking at her eyelid covered with bumps she had exclaimed to herself: "Nice work! I loved that man too much."

Later, recalling the sensation (her eye opened again at Leuven's a short time after), what she identified most clearly in the foreground was her great fear. "If I hadn't been so afraid, it would have been nothing at all, or I would have understood it better." In the same way that in the "stage box" incident the emotion of *shame* was so strong that in truth the stage manager was the product of the shame and had only to appear for Catherine to be delivered over to ignominy, she also bore within her such a great *fear* that accidents like the occlusion of her eye could occur at any time in a dramatic manner.

Indeed, the spasm of the eyelid existed for a long time. For as long as Catherine had not familiarized herself with "the eyes," many phenomena of this sort occurred. She placed eyes on all things. In her real dreams, they were blue and without eyelids, very large, swimming in space. During false dreams and when she was awake, she saw eyes that were generally closed bulge out from one object or another. They were personal eyes: for instance, the eyes of Flore asleep. Or they were "eyes of the dead," with protruding orbs and slits the color of ash. Or the eyes of Pierre, of Pierre from the time past when they would gaze "into each other's eyes."

Thus, once Catherine was climbing a very white, very hard wall. Seeing that it was absolutely flat, one could say of this wall:

$$\text{Radius of curvature} = \text{infinity}$$

and saying this formula: "Radius of curvature = infinity," and saying it again: "Radius of curvature = infinity," Catherine, who was climbing hard up the wall, thanks to the formula and by virtue of the formula *radius of curvature = infinity*, managed to cause *a very old eye* to burgeon upon this wall, incised there, solitary and colorless.

The problem of the wall was posed again another day. Now the wall curved. The eye began to move. Gently, slowly, the eye opens. As though the breath were returning to its lips, it sees again, it is going to know, it will recognize life. It is blue; its expression is indefinable; it belongs to no one, it is without personality. Its extremely powerful gaze has the gift of piercing the most resistant substances, like certain rays that probe life to its darkest depths; and at last the eye, whose action goes so far, swims, it swims drifting on the side in a direction foreseen by itself, and at the very end, oscillating a little, it stops. The eye of Life finds itself in the middle of the flank of the wall that has taken the form and the aspect of a living belly.

* * *

Meanwhile, Catherine Crachat, in reality, is walking toward Joseph Parchemin's bed, in the nursing home in the rue S.

Parchemin no longer had anything left of Parchemin. The trivial personage, with his small, very French mustache, had already disappeared forever. The face of this former traveling postcard salesman, having been enriched with a beard, appeared majestic and dry like a saint's face. One was reminded of a Zurbarán monk impatient to breathe his last. He was between two sleeps, and only the brown glitter of his pupil proved that he existed; he recognized no one. Catherine took the hand on the sheet and squeezed this piece of machinery; in the midst of a significant silence, she definitely had the impression of having been grasped and also stored away by the brown eye. "It's frightfully depressing," she would have liked to say, "the way doomed people look at you."

In a corner, a young person was stamping letters, licking envelopes. She stood up, she greeted Catherine. "Noémi."

At first sight she seemed a sweet and inoffensive creature, peaceful, rather plantlike in type. Standing, she appeared pretty. She was not tall; her face seemed that of a real woman, her body indeterminate and childlike. How old was she? If she was past sixteen, she could be thirty. Despite the mark of tears, her skin was good and pink; she was defending herself firmly against her trials; her wavy hair very black. Her expression was not inane, positively, but asleep. From close up, her features had something vulgar about them.

Catherine felt herself growing weak.

Thus it is, for her, that the need to love begins. She saw her weakness coming very quickly, and she put her arm around the waist of the young girl, who was wearing black clothes in anticipation.

Yes, the rapidity of this onslaught was extreme. Catherine no longer needed to know Noémi's age; Noémi was not yet as old as she would have to be to make her way alone in life, and she would be *the Orphan*. At that moment Catherine was not only drawn to Noémi, but she also felt a collusion with Noémi that did not surprise her in the least. Her dear Noémi was there and was appearing at the appointed hour. Thus, Catherine nudging Noémi, they approached the father together. As though the girl had exhausted her courage, she blinked her eyes continually. And so that the dying man could understand, Catherine raised her arm again and broadly encircled Noémi's shoulders.

. . . No, not only Parchemin, the shadow of Parchemin. The scene was so much larger, the person so much greater! What was the source of the emotion she had, of love mingled with a certain joy at seeing that he was truly going to die? A human person who is dying, even someone of middling importance—shouldn't that make one feel bad? On the contrary, she was not crying. She was happy, and at the same time she was afraid. "The scene I never saw . . . I am seeing it . . . the scene." It was too clear that for

Catherine a person other than Parchemin was involved here; she was aware of it, but she asked herself who, in the same guise as this semblance of a monk, was disappearing before her eyes.

LITTLE X.

When one has had many emotions, one craves emotion. Emotions come running, they are born of the smallest incidents, they emerge, it would seem, from the paving stones of the street. Coming back from the clinic, Catherine went on foot. She had a great deal of walking to do. This passion for walking made her lose hours, but in fact did her no harm, since her time was no longer worth anything; and the locomotion allowed her to remain stationary inside herself with respect to a deep emotion. She found herself in a very dense dark street. An extremely tall street, and so empty that she had to turn her head to the right and the left. Now she heard, in this so very deserted street, a human step. "Someone's going to come up to me and make me a dirty proposition." Her heart reacted sharply to this idea, "even though it would be pleasant to hear if it's really very gross. Just as it's sweet to be pinched in the metro by an ignoble but well-mannered gentleman." But the man's step became fainter as it approached instead of coming near and hardening as she had hoped, and at the same time the step seemed to her completely familiar.

A child touched her on the arm.

The child was not trying to find her way and was not asking for money. She was clinging to her. She did not want to be questioned about why she had come up. And Catherine felt no need to do that. No, Catherine was not waiting for explanations. She was moved and happy: as though something new in her was satisfied. The little girl must have been seven years old. "I'll call her Little X."

They walked a good way without saying a word to each other. But after that they talked.

"You thought it was a man?" said the little girl.

Catherine answered yes.

"People always think it's men."

Catherine smiled, delicately.

"I came to find you again," said the little girl, "because I felt that you needed that."

"Yes, of course," said Catherine. "All the better."

"I know your troubles," said the little girl.

"That doesn't surprise me coming from you." Catherine added, squeezing her hand, "Cunning child!"

She was extremely touched to see the little girl again. She felt younger and as though she were physically larger. And the little girl said mysteriously, "I know a lot through you and a lot through him."

"Who do you mean by 'him'?"

"Leuven, of course." The little girl adopted a solemn tone: "I think you can have confidence in Leuven."

"How reasonable you've become," retorted Catherine.

"Oh, I understand almost nothing outside of you and me."

It would be hard to say what sweetness, what calm Catherine felt in her heart at the thought that she had the Little One's arm in hers. So she began to question her.

"Tell me, what are you thinking?"

"I'm thinking that everything is going very well."

Singular little girl, so close to one, who thinks what one wants her to. But the Little One began to chat volubly, of one thing and another. About this and that. There were stories and more stories, about birds, about bouquets, about hay cut down there on the farm, about attics and about little cupboards.

"Oh you remind me . . . you remind me . . . ," said Catherine, tears in her eyes.

Of the meadows first, and a tree very very very tall, and in the distance very very small forests, a cloud on a bell tower, and the bell tower on a mound—in short, the life on the Savoy farm that Catherine had known so well, since it was her own, but forgotten, and which she would have continued to forget if the Little One had not come to tell her stories, almost the same.

At last the Little One, having unwound her reel, stopped; but she immediately broached a more serious subject.

"You went to the theater the other evening, and there you were accused."

"That's true, who told you?"

"Certainly you must have done something bad for that to have happened."

"And what about you, do you also feel that you have committed a sin?" asked Catherine.

The Little One, under the streetlamp, became whiter than paper. "I feel it."

They were silent.

"They have exposed my guilt before men, women, and children. Though I scorn people, even so, I find that unbearable!"

But the Little One added the key words: "It is inside oneself that it is unbearable."

The Little One created a diversion.

"Then you dreamed about an eye."

"It's quite possible. As soon as it gets dark in a place, I see eyes there."

"Eyes are pretty," said the Little One. "I don't know why that one scandalizes you." She went on: "That's why they always say: you have an eye."

"What are you trying to get at?" sighed Catherine.

"The eye is many things, that's why the eye is pleasant. The eye looks at the tall tree and the small forest, and the eye is also what you have that is most beautiful in your face, since they say: your beautiful eyes."

"Yes, that I know."

"The eye also looks at you when you have done something wrong, when you haven't behaved well. Remember the eye in the triangle with the rays, on the altar."

"Yes."

"But the eye is much better than all that. You know what it is?" The Little One cuddled up, rubbed against Catherine; she was in a strange state, laughed, recovered herself, and buried her head in the fold of Catherine's arm.

"You know what it is? Can you guess?"

She was playing cat and mouse. "Guess, go on. You know? Getting warm?"

In vain, Catherine patted her on the fingers to make her keep quiet. And the Little One squirmed more and more.

"I'm going to show you the eye!" Following an irresistible impulse, the Little One lifted her skirt. When Catherine had seen, everything calmed down and became orderly again. The little girl walked arm in arm with the big one among the lampposts.

V

Joseph Parchemin had died, and the doctors asked that he be subjected to a quick autopsy in the bathroom.

Here was Catherine in the bathroom. How, in the bathroom? Well—lying in the bathtub. Entirely in the bathtub, no, but reduced to a woman's trunk; and not a whole woman's trunk, but rather, to be precise, a woman's belly. Catherine was a female belly, quite precisely, in the bathtub, and next to the bathtub stood a man, a man who was perhaps someone familiar and perhaps no one, for he showed only his back. Yet this back resembled that of a German doctor whom she had known in Bavaria, at the time of the death of her friend Fanny Felicitas. The doctor—for he was one—was actively busy arranging instruments on some velvet in a window; injection syringes in particular, syringes of a fairly large size, she noted. All of this was not very serious, gave an impression of farce. "If he thinks he can do poor Parchemin's autopsy like that . . . " He was meticulously arranging the objects on the garnet velvet and returned to it several times, the better to impress one; but instead, one expected him to set out little signs on it, like a grocer or a pharmacist. Catherine, reduced as she was in the bathtub, saw nothing coming; she got up and went out of the bathroom. Several times she came back, however. "Are you going to begin the autopsy?" But always the same thing, the individual was occupied with the same foolish business. In the end Catherine decided not to return at all anymore; too bad for poor Parchemin's autopsy, but she was too humiliated at being reduced to a belly, and humiliated by this man who was turning his back on her, and more exactly seemed incapable of taking any interest in her, and even more exactly of taking an interest in the belly which she now was.

Little X.'s predictions were therefore not absolutely correct, and everything was not going as well as possible. Then who was the person (singularly alert) who was wondering with such dismal anguish what condition they would leave him in? Vainly did Catherine Crachat declare her perfect goodwill. That is, two voices were speaking at different levels and in different languages about the same single question; in this case, as one may well imagine, the person to whom these inner chidings are addressed no longer knows which way to turn. In the absence of the mysterious Little One, Catherine Crachat offered herself the following reasoning: I am having myself "operated" on by this man Leuven in order to derive a great deal of benefit from it. On the other hand, there are risks in carrying out the operation. How can one continue the operation without incurring the risks, and what do you do to get around this dilemma?

"What do you do to get around it?" "I'm going to go a long way away, I shall cut my ties with the past, I shall change my name, and no one will find me." This was her daydream, whereas she knew very well that, on the contrary, she would have to stay there and figure something out. At that time the only things that occupied her life were her cigarettes and the newspaper. She no longer displayed any elegance; rather, she neglected herself, she did not even keep herself very clean. Flore grew indignant at it, but what was Flore? Catherine, by now completely egotistic, henceforth saw Flore as a sort of good angel whom she badly needed. Catherine, fed by Flore, no longer did anything. Catherine smoked two packs of yellow cigarettes a day and read the paper. She understood, during those long hours, the newspaper's reason for existence. With its succession of depicted catastrophes, the newspaper stupefies the mind, empties the heart, and when one has finished the paper, there is *nothing* left in one's thoughts. When Catherine sought this "nothing," she would plunge into the newspaper. To the point where Flore was disgusted to see Catherine devouring the papers.

* * *

If at least Little X. had been willing to help her! But she did not come back to Catherine. *The Little One*—Catherine surmised—*constituted a mystery.* Catherine was not going to force the Little One's life secret and thus deprive her of her life—which would surely happen. Since her coming had been so real, and the feeling so contagious, to the point where she had left an indelible image in Catherine's heart, why address any sort of challenge to her?

The Little One had left her like everyone else, saying good-bye. Catherine had not been surprised at it; only sad. She knew very well that the Little One was not from her part of town. The next day, Catherine had found in her mail an envelope containing the Little One's photograph. A little girl, standing up, was seen in profile. Her arms and knees were bare. She was wearing a white openwork lace dress, with a full skirt in the back, whose belt was formed of a ribbon knotted with two large loops. On her legs, pretty little white kneesocks. For her head, she had posed full face, her expression seemed beautiful; her cheeks were round, her chin dimpled, her hair was cut in bangs across her forehead. Her eyes—my God, how sad they were. Her eyes were so sad that this child, perched on an upholstered chair in front of a dismal heavy curtain, could have passed for a mature woman of more than forty.

Catherine had kissed the photo, had locked it away and hidden it from Flore. All this made her singularly ill.

STERILITY

Then Catherine entered the dark room once again. The room, the oldest in the aged building in the Maubert area, was built longer than it was wide and down its length was divided by a sort of counter. On the counter, a grille, probably gilded; but, as we said, it was dark in there. Behind the grille a great heap of books seemed to be visible, old books in disorder. The room could belong to a philosopher or a junk man. She could imagine the owner well enough: dirty, with a grubby sweater and vestiges of soup in his beard, busy contemplating some philosophical ideas; but he wasn't there. In front of the grille, no one. On the ground, on the other hand, a black cat.

The cat—was it because of the sadness of the place, the lack of air?—the black cat was almost dead. Flat, odd, crumpled, he was lying there with his paws stiff, and only his eyes were alive in the shadows, greenish and at times pink. What a filthy animal! Catherine said to herself. But Catherine, through a sort of emotion which we all know, received inside herself the order to bring it back to life, and when we say *order,* it really was an order: in truth, the first categorical order that Catherine had ever received.

"Come, let's revive the cat!" But she was afraid: wouldn't it be vicious? And it was all very well to bring it back to life: but how? "You have to blow into its body, that's the best way." Catherine, very disgusted, took the cat between two fingers, by the tail. Truly the tail of a sick animal. So she blew into the tail, and through the tail into the inside of the cat. As she blew, the cat, of course, became fuller and was reinflated.

All of this succeeded in creating a proper cat, we might even say a handsome cat. On his feet, he was purring; he also put his throat against Catherine's bare arm. But *she was tired of it!* And what was more, she still scorned this wonderful cat afterward, just as she had before. So that she took it by the tail again, and brutally, with a thunderous force, sent it flying over the grille, amid the black books. Saying:

"You're good for nothing. Go die!"

"You're Good for Nothing," Catherine recalled, was an episode of a film they had been showing fifteen years ago. It was titled: *Sterility.* It was based on a novel by Mr. Bennett. It was about an old secondhand bookseller infected with greed and married to a woman "still young," and she herself, in fact, had played the woman. The woman, attached to this horrible bookseller, wilts a little more in each scene; the woman is dying of privation, while the bookseller is dying because of a cancer whose manifestations have been taken as the effects of his greed.

The background to the story of Catherine's life up until this point was therefore sterility. Sterility, one may safely venture, is a misfortune that depends solely upon an inner disposition. After having obeyed the order and fully reinflated the cat, she had had to hurl it to the devil so that the act would be sterile.

This time Catherine felt that the main strengths of her being had been awakened. There are insights that form with a singular and incomprehensible authority. There are certainties that nothing can prevent. "Sterility," applied to her, was one of these certainties. Sterility: a single attempt at sexual love, with insufficient satisfactions; sterility: childbirth eluded by efficacious means. Sterility: a failed life as a woman, a failed life as an artist. There was sterility even in the ironic mechanism by which one doubted every operation aimed toward the recovery of health—doubted the order one had received to cure the ill of sterility.

She felt that a complex collection of things was developing badly in her soul. This point was brought into evidence. Catherine accepted that the point should be brought into evidence and that the question of her whole life should thus be fully posed.

VI

If one had searched for an illustration of the orphan (it's a common species, the young girl in deep mourning), one would have found none more representative than Noémi.

Noémi was surrounded by blackness. In it, her pink and puffy face seemed to rejoice with a dark rejoicing. Her face was designed, one would have said, for blackness; her hair, when she put brilliantine on it, had the gleam of a crow's wing. She radiated a black glow tinted by faint colors: pink, green, ivory white.

No, with her papa buried, she had not even the friend of a friend left in the region of Pau; if family existed elsewhere, perhaps, her papa had quarreled with them; the people toward whom Noémi felt affection had arrived unexpectedly at the same time as her misfortune. It was in Paris that she felt best as an orphan; thus she said she would never go back to Pau. Once Joseph Parchemin's body was interred there, she had briskly sold off the house in which everything reminded her of her happiness with "him" after the death of her mother; she had brought back the money, which constituted her only fortune. The poor child bowed her forehead and declared, "I know that my parents' soul is not in Pau."

Hearing this remark, mightn't one think that Noémi was open to the consolations of religion? Not at all. Like everyone, she had certainly received a religious education in accordance with her mother's wishes and against her father's. But she was no longer a believer, especially since the death of her father. Noémi instinctively detested every doctrine or imagination of "the other life." Whether it was in heaven or in hell, if it was *after death* she was horrified by it. Noémi Parchemin, even though an orphan, wanted to experience only our earthly joys. She made her point of view perfectly clear in her description of her father: "He was a Voltairean and he loved women."

Meanwhile, in the apartment of the two women, into which Noémi had crept, she felt quite at ease. She always arrived in the evening. "Madame Catherine embraced her. Mademoiselle Flore would almost have taken her on her knee. Every cloud has a silver lining, since here she is, placed in an advantageous friendship." Noémi, when everything was going well for her, had a birdlike charm. It would have been tempting to call her "wagtail" when she walked, but she was most often seated, her hands occupied with sewing; she says nothing; she listens; she looks from time to time with an affectionate but courageous eye toward her protectresses.

Noémi was not silent, far from it; she spontaneously recounted what she had to tell in order to be better understood. Especially since Madame Catherine, in the melancholy disposition in which she found herself, needed to hear other people's stories. Thus Noémi said that "between her papa and herself, it was completely intimate." During the time that had preceded the illness, in the hotel, they had shared a single room.

"It was nice and pleasant. We were like a married couple, Papa and me, after Maman died. My maman, on the other hand, was a very devout Catholic, and she accepted death very quietly."

Catherine remembered the good Parchemin at the time of Noémi's childhood: skirt-chaser, hard drinker, he had a lively taste for obscenity.

"I was fifteen years old," Noémi confides. "I wanted to become a Carmelite. It's so beautiful to be a Carmelite, because the veil is brown and the robe is white. So I felt I could have been a Carmelite. I wasn't put off by the austerity of it, quite the opposite! But I found that instead my duty was to stay with my parents. I stopped going to church because my confessor tried to forbid me to wear short sleeves. My maman, who was always very sweet, said to me, 'You certainly have the right to wear short sleeves!' But I didn't go to church anymore and that hurt my maman."

Then: "She was unhappy, even though my papa was very good. And me too, between fifteen and twenty, I was unhappy, unhappy, much more so than now."

Noémi smiled, the smile brightened her amiable face.

It appeared that Noémi Parchemin had eliminated love from her life. But she had her friendships. While she was burying her father, she had formed one with which she seemed enchanted. The friend was an old pauper.

"He used to walk all alone, at night, down a street in Pau. He walked all alone, dragging his leg. He had once been a lawyer, but now he was obliged to beg. He begged very discreetly."

Noémi had gone up to him after giving him alms. She had driven him back to his home.

"His room was very dirty. He caressed me on the cheek."

"Oh no!" added Noémi when she understood the feeling of the woman she was talking to, "no, I'm not afraid of anyone."

"All the same," said Flore. "And what happened then, in his room?"

"I heated up his coffee, he drank it, and then I put him to bed on his pallet."

"She's amazing!" cried Catherine, laughing. Since that day, Noémi had been writing to her pauper regularly.

"I went to his room three times without being seen. We talked. His story is a novel, but he made me promise not to tell it."

She sent him money in letters sealed with five red seals bearing the initials N.P. She claimed he was so good, so refined. She said he was able to understand everything. As his friend, she lectured him, declaring to him that he could not remain in the condition of beggar, and she made him promise to make good use of the sums she gave him. "I'm not rich, be careful," she wrote; "this won't go very far." What made Catherine laugh particularly heartily was that she called him "the former lawyer."

After a very short time, Noémi adored Catherine.

THE CLASS

And from the moment that Catherine's different personae, as yet without a sense of their substance and depth, had collectively yielded, the operation took a rapid turn; first, curious perspectives opened on all sides. Obviously, that was all "one" was waiting for. There was a great silence, like a prolonged moment of meditation. Then this story.

The child is four years old, or six. She is a child, a girl, all of whose movements Catherine knows. The child is surrounded by other children of the same age, and together they form a chattering class, in the country school. In the beginning, a rumor.

The Little Girls. They're going to make you do it. You'll go.
The Child. I'll go where?

43

The Little Girls. She's the *new one.* She doesn't know how or what. You'll go, because they're going to ask you questions. Marie-Flower-Pot!

The child looks at the blackboard, which is immense, smeared; and before it stands an imposing figure: for he is dressed as a woman with a stout chest in a blouse "with fob pockets"; he has a crewcut, a brown mustache, and is wearing glasses.

The Little Girls. That's the teacher.
The Child. She's ugly.
The Little Girls. Wait your turn!
The Child. I'm not afraid. I'm not afraid at all!
The Little Girls. They always say that at first. Marie-Touch-Your-Bottom.

The teacher laughs. She agrees with the little girls. Then we hear a shout: "Marie!" The child says to herself: "My name is Marie." She gets up from her bench and goes to the blackboard.

The Little Girls. Teehee! What's she going to take out?

The teacher doesn't move a muscle. She is as if turned to stone. The child feels something in her mouth.

The Child. Here, Ma'am.

The child puts her fingers in her mouth, and she withdraws . . . a dead mouse, which had been tucked inside her left cheek. Upon seeing the dead mouse, the class of little girls laughs—they laugh until they can't hear themselves anymore, such is the amount of noise they are making—and the teacher laughs too, under her breath.

Catherine woke up drenched in sweat, terrified in her heart, because this gave a good indication of what the child's life would be like. It would have been better for that child . . . But right after that there was a hole in the grass, the entrance to a black hole. A little rat comes out, frightened, and pokes her pretty gray nose into the air. Scarcely has she taken a few breaths than one sees her go back in, head first. A few seconds pass; here she is again. And then she goes back in. And then comes out. And then goes back in. And so on for a long time. And then . . . One says to oneself: she's going to come back again. But one never sees her again.

It was then that Catherine suddenly recalled that her father, the medical student, used to call her "his little rat."

* * *

When Catherine left Noémi with Flore that evening, she took refuge in the bathroom, then went to bed; as soon as she was in her bed, the light switched off and black night around her, Catherine felt an almost imperceptibly light touch at her feet; then she received a slight jolt; finally she realized that Little X. was there and was visiting her.

Back again! She had come back.

Little X. showed herself by touching her on one foot, then the other, with extreme delicacy. The room was perfectly black. How favorable it was to the two of them!

"Well, what have you been doing? I didn't see you anymore," said big Catherine.

The Little One, who was touching her feet rhythmically, did not want to answer right away. "Let's let her amuse herself," thought Catherine; and she yielded to the child's chaste caress, so oddly given to her two feet, and found herself comforted by it already. But Catherine was longing to ask another question: "What do you have to say to me?" It was still far too much to ask the Little One. No doubt because of the perfect darkness, the

Little One seemed mute, and who can know what a familiar demon really intends to do? Catherine opted for contenting herself with her presence and was about to go to sleep, when the Little One breathed angrily, "Damned fat mother, have you been drinking, that you don't know I am here?"

"But I do know," groaned Catherine, "I know."

And she indicated that she knew, with her foot; the Little One immediately showed that the foot was giving her pleasure. She said out loud: "True! It's not unhappy. I've been drumming for quite a long time now." She remained full of her resentment and cried out several times, "Shit!" In the end Catherine softened her with a great thrust of her heart; the Little One became polite and kind again. They were going to embark upon an intimate evening together.

"She's definitely a girl from the Compesière farm," thought Catherine, "and she's a *smart girl*."

"Why are you thinking ill of me?" said the Little One immediately.

"Come, let's stop arguing, Little One. We love each other."

"Yes, we love each other!"

Catherine felt the Little One's kiss spread all over her. Then the Little One said, "Your Noémi has gone to bed at last."

"My Noémi!"

"I have no liking for that one myself."

"You're jealous."

"Promise me, by your father's memory, that I will always be more important to you than she is!"

* * *

"Now listen carefully to what I want to say to you. The things that are happening to you now are serious."

"Yes, I'm learning sad things. But," said Catherine, "have I always been so sad?"

"Oh yes, you can be sure of that."

With a different emotion, with a second voice: "You got my picture and you like it very much, right?" With the first voice: "I've always liked playing with mice. The dead mouse is a little child, inside that child; and the child is dead. That's just what I think: one day I will have a child in my body, but you'll see, it will be quite dead."

"That's frightful," said Catherine, crying. "And why?"

"Because of the others: little sister dead, little father dead."

Hearing that, Catherine sobbed heavily into her pillow. So *child* equals *dead.*

Little X. went on in the second tone, more cheerfully: "The story about the rat is a nice one. That one took place near the farm, in the Potru field."

Catherine jumped as though an electric current had passed through her arms and legs. "The Potru field!" She had forgotten that name. And there was the name!

"In the Potru field, you know, one loves to be alive. One loves to breathe the air and look at what shines in the sun. I was watching the rat: in the grass in the Potru field, it was completely like that."

"But tell me, why did she keep coming out?"

"To come out is to come into the world."

"Then that is to come out of my mother." A fresh cloud of tears fell upon Catherine, for she was thinking: according to the story of the Potru field, *earth* equals *death,* but *earth* means *mother,* therefore *mother* also equals *death.*

"Mama," cried Little X. with a cold ferocity, "I killed her!"

"You mean we lost her early."

"Luckily! She used to slap me around under my breast. One day . . . "

The Little One disappeared at three or four in the morning. Catherine, tired from crying, fell asleep. She was warned of all the death she contained.

VII

The pedestal table was made of a blond, vaporous material. It was the table "as I saw it in my great aunt's house." Probably made of gilded wood, it had a leg with three feet and a round top. In truth, the pedestal table had been revealed, so to speak, against the space, for at first in the eyes of the observer there was a space or an abyss without color (if gray can express the absence of color). The gray abyss that did not exist nevertheless assumed a real consistency if one wished it strongly. From being the groundlessness that it was, it became the background; and as it approached in that way, from its substance emanated the pedestal table. If I say "emanated," it was not entirely that; what seemed to happen was, rather, the effect of a piece of psychic work aided by a certain mental tool, and that tool, as it worked the substance of the groundlessness, succeeded, at the end of its effort, in producing a spongy image that was the pedestal table. In fact, there was effort, real effort, with a view to finding and then inscribing in the middle of the sky this word-image-table, which, if it had a three-footed leg and Chinese gildings, was no less, for all that, the *word* of a profound discourse and the expression of its meaning.

On the pedestal table thus created (and which was steeped, it must be said, in a memorial family atmosphere) two objects lay. To tell the truth: the objects came into being at the same time as the table. The first: a candle. The second: a perfectly round eye, expressionless, very moist. A little later, but still linked to the objects, appeared a brilliant spot; was it a flame or only the radiance of a flame? But the three things, linked, let us repeat it carefully, linked and associated through their origins and through their meaning, had to produce a sort of demonstration and end in a piece of evidence. The idea that things exist more and more is expressed, expresses itself and convinces. The idea that they are united convinces even more. The candle is to the right, the eye to the left, the brilliant spot in the middle: *a triangle is formed* in which, overriding fact, the two objects are objects while the spot is not an object; it is, rather, a spirit.

In the course of time Catherine saw the eye again, and the table; but never again with that calm, that august serenity and the character of absolute obviousness. That day, nothing varied, nothing was out of focus, it was perfection. It seemed as beautiful as justice, as happy as eternal happiness, and in a slightly grotesque form it was the holy of holies. All around, were there wings, gusts of wind? A lively, perfumed atmosphere busied itself actively around the table itself, old-fashioned and sacred.

* * *

"Since then," said Catherine, "I have thought a lot about it and believe I knew them all. I often saw the eye again, never the candle. Oh wait—a memory. It's in the rue Jacob. I had just . . . loved Pierre Indemini, when I had the vision of a window in the country, with white curtains, and against the window, to one side, a pedestal table—wait—on the table a candlestick, and in the candlestick there must have been the candle . . . the little globe of fire shone intensely and I found it unpleasant."

It was therefore necessary to succeed in "seeing" that the candle which was shining so strongly was the force of virility with the form it takes in men, since Catherine herself said that that unfortunate candle reminded her of her father, always distracted and with his hat on the back of his head. But then she also had to note that the eye, at first merely feminine, took on "maternal" overtones, and that the pedestal table with its single leg became the support of the family. "You know, I didn't really know the family pedestal table. Of life in Paris I remember almost nothing;

poverty in a hotel room. In the Savoy, when he was earning a little money, I was four years old; they were already ill, he and she. My life was to sit on a step at the Compesière farm, because Madame d'Estiévand, the one who had to serve as my grandmother, had taken me there to save me from the germs. Ah, that d'Estiévand, what a woman! She protected my mother, and she adopted me after their death. My father came to the farm from Saturday to Monday."

Little X. added her two cents' worth by remarking that this was an attempt of Catherine's to reconcile herself with everyone.

* * *

But, God be thanked, the Little One had not met Noémi at the door. This Noémi was so settled in here that when Catherine returned home she had the impression she was returning home to Noémi's place. It was useless to say to her in a very surprised tone: "Hey—is that you, Noémi?" Noémi was not sensitive to this sort of remark.

M. Trimegiste was in the living room.

Trimegiste is in the middle of the living room. He's a very tall man with a massive body. Whether he is standing or sitting, his masculine majesty makes itself felt. This powerful man, even as he utters the polite remarks that one expects of him, is looking at his face in a mirror. M. Trimegiste goes slowly with everything he does. For it would be a mistake to believe that a businessman does things quickly; a businessman does things slowly. Trimegiste's concerns are buildings, jewelry, and insurance. It was as a jewelry broker that he became acquainted with Catherine in the time when she wore necklaces; it was in this form that relations were struck up and that a friendship evolved: "Tell me, now, Trimegiste . . . "—a little service here, a little service there—in such a way that he was made familiar with the complicated part of an artist's existence. M. Trimegiste goes slowly, and, contemplating himself in the mirror, he thinks of his age.

Catherine blinks her eyes as though coming up out of the cellar. She takes Trimegiste to one side and explains: "You don't know Noémi. I'll tell you about her. She's Parchemin's daughter. You remember Parchemin. No? Well, it doesn't matter. She's a pretty child, isn't she?"

What is always pleasant in Trimegiste is the impression of solidity and rationality that he gives us. Catherine cannot manage to understand why, in a dream that is already old by now, she once attributed to him the form of a harlequin and an artist. One can sense that Trimegiste is immediately interested in Noémi. What is more, Noémi does not take her eyes off him. With Trimegiste one is assured of receiving an encouraging response to the proposition one makes. He accepts everything. And along with that he has various other qualities: there are few men as capable as he is of entering another person's skin; he is insinuating, he possesses antennae for feeling out other people's secrets. This leads Flore to say (with her habitual spitefulness) that "he sucks women."

M. Trimegiste is drinking tea.

The conversation is gay because Catherine is eager to escape herself, to come out, to manage to come out of a stifling cellar. But it takes very little to recall you to reality. For instance, Noémi, who has moved away from them a little, keeps changing the way she looks. Catherine would like to point out to Trimegiste the astonishing physical transformation of which Noémi's appearance is capable. Truly, Catherine says to herself, there is not one of her, but several. Just look at what has been going on for a few minutes now. She does not stop changing. One doesn't know if it's because of her mood or of events that affect her.

Noémi's person number one is, in society, an unbreakable doll-twin; at these times she is smooth and nice. But a mere nothing swells her, she inflates; now she is a young prostitute whose eye and hand are already full of experience. If the motion continues, there appears Noémi number three, the worst: a blackish green creature, a suicide. One then sees Noémi number four, who is a beautiful, frigid young woman, with a serious face, scornful of the preceding personages; here, her head is a good twenty years older than her body. This evening, Noémi keeps going from number two to number four to number three, and she moves with dizzying speed. The fact is that Catherine has said to Trimegiste "that once she dreamed he was a painter and was painting Noémi's portrait."

Noémi utters the following sentence: "I have no ambitions for either fame or wealth," and repeats it twice. This sentence has its full effect on the people listening, and Noémi falls silent.

M. Trimegiste would like to hear other sentences, just as beautiful, from Noémi. He questions her about what she likes. He asks her to say "what she wants to do in life." Noémi, even though she is in mourning, loves dances, literature, walks in Saint-Cloud. In life she will be "a secretary." To come back to the dances, she goes only to the ones that are *proper*. Trimegiste's questioning becomes urgent: "Do you go to them alone?"

"No, monsieur, I go with Marie Touchant."

"Marie Touchant!" exclaims Trimegiste. "Who is she?"

"She's one of my friends. She is alone at the moment. She lives at 32, rue Cujas, in case you want to know."

It seems now that answers are being torn from Noémi in her persona number three. Catherine sees Noémi's misery. She can picture to herself her painful falseness. Catherine would like to slap Trimegiste, in defense of Noémi. But Noémi yields to the temptation, answers, and in this way he takes possession of her.

"Yes, Marie always makes me laugh. When we were keeping vigil over my poor papa in the chapel, she made me laugh even that day. Marie nudged my elbow because the sister who was reciting the prayers was squint-eyed and both her eyes were touching her nose." After the death of each parent Noémi heard a little bird, each time a little bird. The bird after her mother's death was a cheerful bird, which sang with delight. But after her father's death, there was another little bird; it was a sad, mournful bird. Noémi doesn't dare say that this was natural or supernatural: she notes it. She also saw bouquets of flowers crossing the room on a diagonal.

M. Trimegiste takes more and more interest in this odd Noémi. Catherine makes a series of observations. Noémi is sitting on a low chair. Noémi has pretty legs, she wears real silk stockings in order to have a delicate calf. Since the hem of her dress comes down to her knees (over her knees when she moves) and she is not keeping her legs together, the result is that the flesh of her thighs is visible to anyone who finds himself in the axis, and such is precisely Trimegiste's position. Noémi is therefore apparently granting a certain view of her intimacy to M. Trimegiste, and this is why the latter is fascinated. Trimegiste does not take his eyes off Noémi on her chair, and Noémi must know what she is doing, because fairly regularly, without changing her position, she pulls on her dress so as *not to cover* her knees.

"How I'd like to know what it is that attaches me to that *girl!* I don't respect her, she is not my type. She bores me. And I am prepared to endure all the preposterous things she does or is going to do, and all her conniving. The patience I have with her . . . I don't understand anything about it. Well, where does her power come from? She is manipulating all of us. The idiot always knows what has to be done and knows in detail the psychology around her. Does she perhaps have the gift of second sight, does she know how to cast spells? No, in fact I think she's perverse. She lives at the level of what you know about, she has remained there, hypnotized like a cat. But wait! On the other hand look at that lovely, pure forehead, that clean complexion, Noémi's sweetness, her reserve. These qualities are not invented. We're not seeing trompe l'oeil here. My preceding supposition was abominable and I believe in Noémi's virtue."

Meanwhile, M. Trimegiste, completely absorbed, leaves the room at Noémi's heels.

VIII

The period of calm did not last in Catherine's heart. The lower forces resumed their domination. Night fell again. She forgot Noémi and the others. Where and when did this take place? With whom?

Toward evening a street extends through a dark, sordid neighborhood. A street which by its dimensions, by the sinister inequality of the houses, the spacing of the lampposts around which the fog drifts, resembles, with its odd line, a presentiment of misfortune. Here is Catherine Crachat. She is walking briskly, as one might imagine at such an hour, in such a neighborhood. However, she is not the only one walking, and many people are slipping by very quickly in both directions. Those shadows go straight ahead without ever turning back. The sky is low over the city like a cover. Everyone files by rapidly, skillfully. They are dressed in black. Catherine Crachat passes alongside a warehouse, but in fact is it a warehouse? It would be lofty if it were not rather low-lying, and its walls, at the point where they meet the asphalt, are so dirty that one would not want to touch them. This sordid building, quite in its place in such a dark neighborhood, could easily be a morgue, but on the contrary, through a sudden reversal of its function, it's a maternity hospital. Here mysteriously full women arrive in troops to undo their bands and deposit their children. Without any doubt she will go in here too, enter this building, on the appointed day and even any minute now, for everyone in this neighborhood does what he is supposed to do. As she says these words, she looks and what does she see? Lost in sleep and sure of being in a mother's arms, a little child whom she is holding against her. True, she can see only his head and his *golden hair,* but how beautiful he is! And she can't help addressing a thought of gratitude to divine Providence, for he is so beautiful, so divine, that she thinks she is holding the son of God! And to complete the picture, a woman whom she doesn't know approaches from behind and places on Catherine's blouse a false breast of porcelain with which she will be able to suckle this child.

. . . Meanwhile, one watches an immense film being shown, of living images as large as life, several reels in scope, of a cartoon-strip type also. The first reel is obliterated, the second too, but at the end of this one Madame d'Estiévand is sitting, old and authoritarian, in a low chair. Catherine, having arrived with her in the great city of Paris, served her as adoptive daughter, nurse, and principal chambermaid all at the same time; and, as it happened, Madame d'Estiévand was busily cutting in half, with a pair of silver scissors that never leave her belt, each grape on an enormous bunch of grapes. Following the rest of the film, further on, one encounters a beautiful bakerwoman: this woman, particularly stoutly built, is behind her counter and performs admirably; this woman gives little Catherine sweet-smelling brioches, very nourishing, "for the trip." But does Catherine need brioches? Since she is going to miss the train? The pastry shop in question is in the rue du Mont-Blanc at . . . (the Fuchs *pâtisserie,* near the station), in the place where Little X. was so perfectly happy listening to the Easter bells, as she recounted it to Catherine . . . The pastrymaker absolutely wants to stuff the brioches into her bag. Then Catherine moves off, passes quickly, and in another part of the page of images—for it won't be said that this business of the grapes and this business of the brioches, of bread and wine refused, will make her impotent forever—in another part of the page of images, she takes a knife from the table, passes a man in the street, and *wham!* she sticks the knife into his buttock.

Masculine, aggressive, there she is! It's the reversal of the first movement.

MATERNITY

But the same street extends through a dark and sordid neighborhood, at the same twilight hour, and the same *it is necessary* is pronounced in an interior manner by an aphonic voice: it is necessary to enter the warehouse. A woman walking behind her has put in her arms a young child whom she suckles, using a false breast.

It is therefore a dark city in which the busy and indiscernable people file in every direction, and some walk to the right and the others walk to the left and the others cross breadthwise, and in the middle of it all Catherine is the only one who is motionless: because it is necessary, the interior voice says to her, to enter the warehouse. The warehouse is in fact the lowest and most wretched of the houses Catherine can conceive of at this solemn moment. What is more, she discerns through the walls the inhabitants of the hovel; as though it were possible, when one makes use of the "interior" gaze, to find oneself inside and outside at the same time. But the door is half-open. Catherine approaches: the door opens wide. A very handsome creature, an adolescent, *with golden hair,* tall in stature, whose face is the *covering* of a heavenly fire, holds the door panels, and with his head gives her to understand, with a careless sweetness, that it is indeed she who is at this moment expected. "So they are expecting me," thinks the visitor, and sweat covers her forehead and pallor invades her cheeks because of the precipitous withdrawal of the blood; but she would not be able to say whether she is led by the natural exercise of her will, or whether, her will struck with terror, she is being forced to go to the place where she is expected.

The divine adolescent is dressed in dazzling, colorless silk. The adolescent's face is no one's face. Very slowly Catherine enters and follows a corridor that ends, finally, in a low room.

Here, stretched out on a slate table, a table arranged for this sort of spectacle, is a very large dead Christ. He is recognizable by his head (though covered with a veil) and his pierced limbs. The adolescent son of light has disappeared in the midst of all this. Catherine realizes that they are intimating to her the order to open the body of this Christ to see what is inside it.

By turns in front of and behind him, Catherine comes up close to the head. A woman larger and stronger than she, with an atrociously determined air, brings the saw and hammer, the utensils for watering. A man dressed in trunks and an apron exercises the authority in this place; he begins to pry open the rib cage. But this frightful sacrilege must be prevented from happening! Catherine, already emotional from so many ordeals, tries to stop them. In order to stop them she attempts to bind *her own* elbows together behind her. But here are two little persons; seated, in perspective, they replace the large, mean woman of the beginning. It is Parchemin, the publicity agent, and the Negro dancer Josepha Backer, but in truth, also, when she turns her gaze on them, the gaze that peers into the human conscience, she sees that they are at the same time her old lover, Pierre, and Flore, the woman she lives with. Thus, she maintains a breathless and cunning silence. "I know from experience," says Josepha Backer, "that the autopsy of a little child is an easy thing. But can one open up an older man, like Christ?"

At this dramatic point, Catharina dares to look at Christ, whose thorax has been cut open; her surprise is boundless when she hears *him speaking*. The voice has an impossible character, since it is both soundless and without timbre, is weaker than a breath of air in a cellar. He is saying, "They have pierced my heart, now they are going to tear out my pulmonary artery." He says this, and as he utters these words, one sees the two bare organs floating in the right side of the chest; and then, when he has said it, the cloth that was covering his holy face begins to slip little by little toward the upper part of his head. Catharina, transported by love and terror, observes what is going to happen! She awaits the appearance of his features, which will follow that of his beard. Alas! Here is almost all of the face. It is a face one has always known. It is mediocre. I will even dare to say it is stupid. And what is Catharina looking at? The simple face of a dead man.

IX

Neither Leuven nor the Little One could release Catherine from the terror that weighed on her. To have failed Christ this way! She went about henceforth like a somnambulist, preoccupied by this idea and completely concentrated in a sort of profound absence remote from real life.

Catherine kept seeing the different sizes again: the little child, natural size; the luminous adolescent and the female anatomist larger than nature but indistinct; the small and distinct persons like Parchemin and Josepha Backer; and Christ, larger than all of them. She went around repeating, "Christ was larger than all of them." She felt an abominable pain. It was because, for the first time, the feeling "It is necessary" conflicted profoundly with the feeling "I can't." Or it was because in the moment when it had been necessary to look inside what she thought was the largest, all of this had become ugly before her eyes. But there was something else much worse. *Who* precisely was this Christ?

She began crying violently, for these reasons. She continued to cry when these reasons disappeared. She went out at night to cry in comfort. She let her tears flow fully and as they liked, over her cheeks, against her neck, down to her chest. Outdoors it was sultry, in summer: but what should she do with the summer? If Noémi was sticking to her and following her like a dog, then it was impossible to cry in a natural way. The last activity Catherine displayed was employed in throwing Noémi off her trail, in order to be able to cry in the streets.

This grief eventually came to touch its opposite, which was anger and resistance. Catherine had entered the path of grief in which submission and revolt share the same nature. She walked on first at the side of the path, which offers resistance, she so feared that the middle would cave in. Leuven claimed she was trying to run away. That overwhelmed her for a truly sad interval, and she conceived a strong aversion for him because of his blunder.

What is happening? What is happening? It is less and less possible to reestablish the natural course of her heart after each attack. Calm seems out of reach, out of sight. Fear dominates. Fear listens to no argument. One can't affect fear either with one's will or with one's reason. When I think with fear without perceiving any cause, without thinking any image, I am in prison inside myself, and it would be better, then, for a blow from outside to knock me unconscious than for a discourse to speak to me. But also, fear questions me: What is the *horror* of that voice? *They* pierced my heart . . . *They* are going to tear out my pulmonary artery . . . What am I when that voice is heard? Am I the guilty one who opened the body? *Was it my fault he died?* Or am I the dead body, in itself? . . . That, in my intention, I killed my father and killed myself with him? That idea is related to what I am feeling.

Now here is my heart's problem. There is so much death in my life: do I indeed want to live, or to die? Am I perhaps already dead? I would accept that. I am shivering. I am shivering.

Comfort me.

* * *

Then she found herself in an enormous crowd, a crowd of derby hats and frock coats, people standing on all sides, the meaning of all this being incomprehensible to her. Why had they come in such numbers? Among these people she felt she was distinctly shorter, and consequently stifled. If one looked closely, one saw that the crowd was composed of photographs that were all the same—except for one real man, taller, in the middle.

The Taller Man [to Catherine]. Come. [Silence.] Come.
Catherine. I can guess. You are a god. [She laughs.] You are a Buddha. [She grins.]
The Taller Man. Come. I'm going to grow taller.
Catherine. I'm the shortest, unfortunately, but I'm slipping through, I'm coming, wait.
The Growing Man. Are you there? Have you passed into me? Have you reached the inside of my body? [Impossible to know whether Catherine succeeded in incorporating herself or not.]

But the next day she was standing among the crowd, still the same, in front of a door that was about to open. They were still wearing derbies and frock coats. She was once again smaller than all of them. The door: behind the door was someone about to die. She was preparing herself for this painful sight. The door opened. Two bedrooms; it wasn't in the first, it was in the second. The second had a country window and the bed was to the left. "Who is that man who's going to die? It seems it must be Trimegiste. How like a demon he looks."

Hermès Trismegistus. Come. [One can barely hear him.] Come.
Catherine. You are all black, I hate you!
Hermès Trismegistus. [Weaker] Come.

Quickly, not knowing what she was doing, Catherine slipped

into Trimegiste's body before he died.

As soon as that horror had ended, Little X. interrupted and said to Catherine: "But don't you remember the bedroom?"

"Oh wait, wait . . . "

"The bedroom where Father died."

"Where *my father died!*" The wallpaper, the window with its white curtains, the bed to the left, of mahogany, with a quilted cover. "Yes. Yes. Yes."

"In the village of Compesière."

"I can see him again, dead, on that bed."

The Little One began again: "I'll bring you other images. Oh, how colorful they are! There's a little girl seen from the back. That's me. In the village square there are three trees. The square is all gray with dust and the trees are yellow. On the ground, dust. I am seen from the back and *you* are looking at me, you see me from the back."

"It's true."

"We have the impression they've made us leave the house because of *what is happening there.*"

"Oh," said Catherine, "yes. It's true. I see it." Catherine remembers well. "I know it really happened, and from now on I will be *that,* nothing else, and I will be it forever, the other life will never come back again. I know I will be able to carry this image and this feeling everywhere in my life, they will be the same as today, everywhere I am and as long as I shall live. No, I don't want to be afraid anymore. I will turn out to be very proud: I am a real orphan. They will all be buried tomorrow morning."

* * *

"Try to understand, then," added the Little One. "These are all memories that make us aware. Deep inside you there's something that doesn't want to live, and always wants to die. Since 'he' senses that he's going to be brought back to earth to live, he is furious. He is searching, as you can clearly see, for dodges by which to save himself. First he says to himself: why not in a god? So as to go higher up? Then 'he' imagines going into some devil of an ordinary man whom you don't like, in order to go farther down. But always, in his mind, it is in order to die. And so always, for us, dying recalls real dying, it recalls the death of our father. And you can already see that everything is confused, like posters glued on top of one another: the father here, the mother there, your child if you ever have one, and the love of Jesus Christ, and everything, it's in death, nothing but death, it is death!"

The Little One paused. "And I believe you've had enough of the operation, that it's costing you too much. *We do not want to live.*"

<h1 style="text-align:center">X</h1>

Yes, enough; she didn't want any more of it. She swore she still consented but that it was impossible for her to go on. She added that he could not *want* her to suffer this much.

"You say that if I am beginning to be reluctant, it's because the old condition of things is fortifying itself so as not to be demolished. You tell me that deep down I want to go on and I can't help wanting it, since here, inside me, *truths* have been touched. I can't answer you; I counter you with two certainties: my suffering, and the idea that it's impossible.

"Oh no, I don't want any more of it! Leave me in peace. I regret—everything that has happened. I no longer believe in any of your explanations. All that—empty nonsense! Nonsense, my dear sir. Nothing in it. *There was never anything in it.* At present we are no longer talking, we are quarreling: a fact that demonstrates that I've had enough. All in all, what you're engaging in is a police activity. You search, you spy, you poke around, you interpret. You lock us up inside your constructions. Your favorite argument is a dilemma. Let me think about the value of your logic. Let me also think about the honesty of your mind. And your heavy Jewish face, reminiscent of certain kinds of cheese, aids you in getting others to believe in the invulnerability of your knowledge, and that everything that happens is part of your plan. You have really tired me out, but you haven't had me. A man who moves about, the way you do, within such embarrassing subjects, who claims to be smart, but never to have real intelligence, because he doesn't have real intelligence, can never be loved. I have tolerated you, nothing more; now I can't tolerate you. Why, why should I tolerate you? How will I profit from this blasted operation? The man who was my life's happiness no longer exists. So? You—what do you have to add? At first I submitted, yes, it's true—why? You say—in order to be able to work again and earn money. In order to have money! Oh, perfect! Your explanation is as dirty as money. Anyway, I can earn money without putting myself in your hands. Yes, but I could no longer manage my work very well, you tell me, or earn the proper amount of money, and according to you I would earn less and less if I did not put myself in your care, but on the other hand they give the big prizes to the ones who develop their skill completely, so that I will eventually, you tell me, be in the situation of one of the best artists. One of the best artists, what does that mean, since I don't care one hoot about art or your operation? Before, I had a love—let's say he was a shade—and I loved him. I had a friend too, and she loved me. But I don't love anyone anymore and no one loves me anymore. *And I don't have the strength anymore,* you understand, I no longer have the strength to kill the people who sit on my face, who place their butts on my face, and whom I hate! I would like to cut them and burn them, those people, particularly a certain fat Jew sitting behind me. But since I no longer have the strength, I have to, I have to, and . . . let me cry.

"The pain . . . with which you have loaded me down . . . is a block. The pain . . . is a block, with which you have loaded me down.

"You claim you can read hieroglyphs! You also remain impassive. At first nothing guarantees that you may not be an impostor. But look out! The block of pain that you have made can't be borne. My tears change nothing about it; the block is too heavy for me. You're the one responsible. You should be dragged into court. You have diminished me; you have plunged me into my own unhappiness. What I used to call 'myself' is, it seems, a lie disguising death, corruption, a love of death. And everyone will understand very well, now, that I am a lie!—no, still not enough!—that I am nothing! Is that what you want to achieve? You are a criminal who must be attacked before the law.

" . . . Let me run away. Permit me to mend, by myself, the harm you have caused me. And what about me, what harm have I done you? Here they come again, these stupid tears."

SPARRINGS

Catherine sprang into a new position, and then fortified herself there energetically.

The point was to be sufficient unto herself and to amuse everyone else. The point was, as she whirled about, to fill the emptiness. The point was to disguise that nothingness with an appropriate attitude. She had to rise above her failure, which was so bitter to her pride, by cultivating her high spirits, her wickedness. For two weeks she was truly infernal.

She told Trimegiste she wanted to have dinner with him every night, and every night in a different spot, and gad about wherever he might like.

"Ah! Good!" he said. "You're abandoning your fits of sifting through old shit. I'm delighted. Believe me, my dear friend, we all contain horrors. The art of living consists in forgetting them. As for the honest man, the sociable man, he holds firmly to a position established on moral values."

"Yes," answered Catherine, "I will go out with you, but on the condition that we make a threesome with Georgette."

"Georgette! My dear . . . Uh . . . Georgette . . . "

What had come over her, to want to resuscitate Georgette? Georgette . . . Georgette . . . She wanted Georgette. Georgette Labutin had been Trimegiste's mistress.

"Yes! All right! Georgette."

She was almost dancing with joy. There were a number of things Trimegiste wanted to explain, that he wasn't getting along with Georgette at all anymore, and that Georgette was an intolerable girl, foolish, don't you see . . . and that he would be delighted, instead, to cure Catherine all by himself—but there was nothing to be done, Georgette was necessary, Georgette was called at once. At the same time, she got Noémi all worked up. "Tell me what you want, all your stories, your seamy little passions, go on, I love it." She established a special sort of intimacy with Noémi. Nothing but innuendo. Noémi responded immediately. Or rather, Catherine's ordinary persona remained at the proper distance, Noémi's persona likewise, while the other Catherine advanced violently on Noémi, summoned her to unlace her corset and be vulgar, like a servant at a dance, which the other Noémi accepted right away. And finally Catherine plotted with Noémi to create a Trimegiste-Noémi bond, "which would make Georgette explode": but then it was necessary to make contact with Georgette for it to be real fun.

During the negotiations, Noémi was in the hallway. "*She* has only to ask the least thing of M. Trimegiste and immediately he is at her feet. Is she ever lucky! Who is Georgette?" Noémi said to herself.

Trimegiste went off.

"She'll be coming with us too!" cried Catherine, crossing her legs. "I'm going to have a good time watching all of you!" What hot, black demon had settled inside Catherine: she had fire under her eyelids—just look at her.

And Noémi, wanting to be protected, clutched M. Trimegiste's hands.

Trimegiste arrived one evening accompanied by Georgette, who was the well-proportioned, carefully polished woman whom everyone has heard of and seen on all the sidewalks. Next to that woman Catherine felt like "Zeus's daughter," but with an inexpressible melancholy.

"I didn't want to go against you," said Trimegiste as a sort of excuse.

And the dear daughter of Zeus: "We know, we know; it's very crass. But just take a look in the antechamber, my dear friend, you who are so busy making eyes at Noémi."

Indeed, Monsieur Trimegiste's stare had become soft and oily when, noting that Noémi was dark while the other was blond, Noémi had seized the opportunity by "the hair" and asked him with her natural impetuosity, flicking a glance at Georgette: "That's your daughter, isn't it?" Trimegiste had felt very happy. He covered Noémi with a gaze that disturbed her very much.

* * *

With Trimegiste, one generally had dinner at the Boeuf and then danced at Kikikoff's. Catherine was in the middle, sometimes having Noémi on her right, Flore or Georgette on her left, or not Flore, or not Georgette, or neither Georgette nor Noémi, or neither Flore nor Noémi nor Georgette, but strangers, and across from her Trimegiste had one or two of his men friends, or no friends at all. The light was very treacherous and, what one saw in it was baroque and sinister. Flore didn't come often and, if she came, she would fall asleep. Noémi refused to come most of the time. Georgette, an heiress from a good family (the Labutins had a bank in the business district), oriented herself decidedly toward "the surroundings"; thus she was there not so much in order to please Trimegiste as to show off her merchandise, which was of good quality. Whereupon, what conversation!

Not all of this was real. The women in furs undeniably had the feel of a nightmare, in their saffron color and their slow motions. As we know, on warm nights Paris smells of the sewer and seems to have a ceiling over it. Georgette displayed her wolfish teeth in response to everything. This rational animal also clawed the mahogany and leather with her red nails, and with her eyes she made concrete propositions to the men. Noémi, on the contrary, still seemed to be from the country and talked about literature. Catherine's private life, warm and painful, was in the orchestra: torn to shreds by the percussion instruments and reworked, by now disgusting, by an interminable saxophone. All of this badly done, badly real. They couldn't escape it. The unfortunate Labutin imagined that Catherine was working on Trimegiste, whereas Catherine had known Trimegiste for about ten years! But this was why she was attentively seeking out Catherine's weak points in order to sink her barbs into them. Alas, there were too many: the girl found nothing.

All the same, Catherine intended to scold Trimegiste about the delicate matter of Noémi's inheritance.

"She has just come into a small inheritance, unhoped for, deriving from a litigation Parchemin had left: forty thousand francs."

"I beg your pardon," corrected Trimegiste, "thirty-two thousand."

"Oh, you're aware of the figure."

"Yes, once all costs are paid, she will have no more than between thirty and thirty-two thousand coming to her."

"I see you're well informed."

"My God, yes, I'm looking after this business. A *small* inheritance devolving upon a charming girl, poor and without support, excites my imagination. What is she going to do with it?"

"But she must invest it properly!" said Catherine, and she was startled to hear herself talking like this, for she had an innate horror of savings and investments.

"Well, well," Trimegiste remarked, "is this then how you react to the thing?"

"Yes," Catherine replied passionately, "this is how I react! If Noémi wants support she has only to ask me for it."

"In any case," said Georgette disdainfully to Trimegiste, "I wouldn't advise the girl to go to you for help, since, if she did, she would soon be broke."

Trimegiste was pleased. Clearly, the two women's attacks delighted him.

"The sum in question," he said, "is laughable, it is *childish,* if one can say such a thing, and must be put to the best possible use. If I am taking an interest in the matter, the only satisfaction I derive from it has to do with the fact that Mademoiselle Noémi, as she assured me, is very attached to that small amount of money."

"It's Noémi's only money."

"Then I will say that Noémi is present for me in her money. You can see that consequently I am considering only the good of your protégée."

"This *little* money is taking on considerable importance for you!" said Georgette ill-naturedly. "Another one I feel sorry for!"

Trimegiste touched Catherine's foot with his own under the table, and smoked his cigar for a long time.

When Catherine returned home, tired of her disgraceful apathy and having drunk too much, she found a letter from Noémi by her bed. It began: "Great friend, my dear, my goddess . . . " and then two pages, or three, of declarations and gossip. In the girl's spirit, Catherine represented lofty principles. Far above the earth floated Catherine, ethereal, incarnating the gifts of the heart and mind, but, alas, insubstantial and beyond the reach of the very humble Noémi! Never, never would Noémi be able to reach her. Such a womanly nature would always elude her! She would never succeed in giving herself completely—she, Noémi— to so mysterious a personality. Noémi often appears foolish in Catherine's presence; she is well aware of it, and she accepts it. It's that Catherine's mind dazzles her so; and in fact she cannot stop herself from blinking her eyes, which makes her seem even more foolish. If Catherine speaks, Noémi is confused. If Catherine is silent, and especially if she shows her sadness, Noémi is overcome with love. Well, she needed to confide *all that* to her dear big sister; the two of them are sworn friends.

Catherine immediately tore the letter into a hundred small pieces. She did not know why, but she felt a huge resentment against everyone, and particularly against Flore. She reviewed in her memory, once again, the episodes of the "maternity hospital" and the "pedestal table." She longed for Little X., but the latter had gone far away.

* * *

Catherine knew perfectly well that she was running a risk by going to this fancy dress ball. Since each person had to represent something at it, she was going to descend still lower on the dismal ladder she had been climbing down, and she would arrive at *the lowest point.* Then she would meet someone there who wanted-ed to make her acquaintance and whom she had until now kept at a distance, instinctively, but whom she no longer had the courage to reject, now that she had arrived at this state.

She comforted herself with the argument that the things of the outside world are *fated* and that, if one hasn't been able to free oneself from them inside, it is better to abandon oneself to them. She would wear a black, hooded cloak and a velvet mask, and would arrange herself so as to be completely invisible. No one would see anything of her but her chin and her breast.

Borne along by fortune, Catherine was taken to the salons of the Clar. As she drove through the shining, empty streets, she swore she would extricate herself from this bad situation and return to Leuven's the next day. Yet she was wearing the black cloak. That she had changed her feeling of "punishment" into its opposite, arrogance and provocation, as she had done, no longer seemed to her a good thing. "The femme fatale was clearly finished; if one examined reality closely, she had never succeeded in being that woman." And she still resembled that woman in the black cloak!

Trimegiste had come as a Romantic poet with a red vest, a Théophile Gautier figure. Flore as Cleopatra and Noémi as "Virginie" were very successful. The dark houses shrugged their shoulders at these accoutrements, and Catherine was disgusted before she arrived.

She had to drink her cup to the dregs, now she was looking for those "dregs." Here, sables were draped over the shoulders of fake women, and armors and plumes came into contact with the nudes of Josepha Backer; the world, history, people surrendered with delight to the confusion. They moved about through the sizzling of several orchestras. On a hot griddle, particles come and go, cling together deliberately, push each other away, marry. Thus the automatic dancers—now forward, now backward—coupled one to the other, and separated once the thing was finished. She had created a sensation as a black object, a hidden woman. Tutankhamen and the Queen of the Belgians circled around her. Policemen, fortune-tellers asked their usual questions, as they looked at her. Fat Margot and some Romans stopped, and even Napoleon I, with Madame Réjane, who was in a pearl-gray tailored suit with leg-of-mutton sleeves and a divided skirt, and was holding onto her bicycle. Lastly, side by side with dairy-men from the suburbs, realistic girls paid no less attention to the black-hooded cloak. Catherine was immediately exasperated by it. What was inside her, anyway, that made her instantly become the center of this pandemonium? She separated the groups. She was of course looking for the back. Shaved armpits give off just as much smell as hairy ones, and one yearned for the emergency window. There were women displaying the lower half of their bodies the way one normally shows one's face, and this thing which stood to reason, as natural as natural history, further added to the weight of the atmosphere. Certain people tried to discover her eyes behind the mask, which seemed to Catherine absolutely intolerable. Yet how was she to drive them off? They weren't flies. From time to time she caught sight of Noémi in the distance; the latter had fooled her friends and was a great success. Théophile Gautier was holding her close. Flore had disappeared: she was pos-ing for the photographer. Georgette was involved in changing sex.

"What is this somber black cloak, so mysterious, so morbid?"

"It is I, Monsieur. *Noli me tangere,* as the apostle said. Go on, clear out. That woman breathes the plague. Yet her character is gentle, imaginative; she suffers. The black cloak moves forward, the silky and magnificent expression of death. It is impressive. It has arrived in the center, and it casts a circular glance of fury over the swayings, the wrigglings, and the genital penetrations of the dance. Even though strange bells are ringing at its forehead, announcing an imminent loss of consciousness, it prepares to take up its little trumpet to make everything collapse and cause the ceiling, falling on the dancers, to drown the masquerade in blood!"

But what does she see and what does she do? Nothing of the

sort. Flore, clearly recognizable behind the mask of Cleopatra, pulls her from this terrible situation in which she was going to do something desperate! Pulls her, pushes her, forces her to walk; leads her to a peaceful corner in front of a gentleman positioned there to wait, a gentleman dressed in a wrinkled Great Mongol costume.

"That man there," Catherine said to herself, "is not part of the ball. He came here for me."

The man's face, uncovered, was sallow. He seemed moved; he had the crudest sorts of features. The role of Mongol suited him well, because of his sinister gravity. His eyes shone with a continuous and subdued gleam, as though he had had a fever. He was smiling. When he smiled, one realized how much distinction his oblique wariness had been hiding. Flore introduced him.

"Monsieur Luc Pascal, writer."

The name of this writer did not penetrate Catherine's hearing, and Flore had to start over again. M. Pascal smiled more; at that, Catherine noticed that there actually was something Asiatic in his expression. At the same moment, she learned that Pascal was in this place, at this hour, solely in order to meet her.

"I wonder why you have gone about it this way," said the black cloak. "It is easier, and more natural, to find me at home."

"I never felt that my wish to see you at home was *necessary* enough," said M. Pascal in a colorless voice. "That is why I have waited for the opportunity for several years."

"You have waited several years to see me?"

"Several years."

Catherine put out her hand. He kissed it with a certain voracity.

SEARCH FOR THE AGGRESSOR

XI

The well of tears is a large well. It's a deep well, an eternal well.
Others besides Catherine have drowned in it forever.

After leaving Luc Pascal, she had given in to it; for eight days
she had surrendered completely, remaining in bed and refusing
help and food. She had been wanting these tears for too long.
How many tears she contained, to see them flow this way!

She leaned over the well.

No one can say where the bottom of it is, black water of sorrow. Pain and death come together there. Leaning over the hole,
she felt, physically, that she was *leaning* for hours and hours. And
that black water, too, had once before come out of her eyes. The
tears descended the length of the tube of rock. By leaning very
far over, she saw not only the bottom of the water of tears, or
death, but other things along the way: privation, misery, fear.
Phantoms inhabited the well of sorrow; their forms kept drawing
you. How to resist the summons? "We are the norms of your life.
Make a small move, take up a weapon, you will accelerate the
inevitable process and you will be delivered."

Sometimes a horrible repose. "I'm all right. I've reached the
end. I can't go any lower."

If she happened to think, again, "what evil have I committed?"—the tears gave her the answer, which is a piece of knowledge. The power of tears lies in the fact that they link physical
pain and moral pain. There is unity. Then one experiences the
utmost comfort in a fierce delight: "I want to suffer. I want to
cry. I will never cry enough."

"I believe," said M. Luc Pascal, who saw Catherine once during this period, and even though, by a prodigious burst of energy, she kept her eyes dry in his presence, "I believe you are abandoning yourself to the pleasure of the massacre of the
innocents."

On one of these days she saw *the Chinese man.* The Chinese man must be described. During this period when she could not put up with anyone's company, she was leafing through the illustrated magazines. The fashionable review *Bateau ivre* gave her what she needed. In the middle of it—the Chinese man. The head of a Chinese martyr. That man's face covered the entire page, right out to the edges.

What precision in the rendering! No wound is visible because it was the *body* that was tortured; but one sees in every feature, every wrinkle, in all the nuances of the open eyes and the rictus, the psychological effect and the emotion that accompanied the death throes.

Ugh! Catherine wanted to throw the paper away; she couldn't. Her dismay took on the force of a hurricane when she noticed that the wretched man's expression was not that of horror. He . . . was not crying. Around that open mouth, which expressed such prolonged anguish, there reigned a sort of happy delicacy, felicity . . . beneath the drops of sweat, of blood . . . there was a heavenly joy.

Ah, double horror! It was magnificent. Catherine began to speak. "No, I can't look at that." "Yes you can, show it, show it, one more time." "But I can't look at that!" "Show it again!" It was so hideous; how frightened she was. "What do you want me to say, Chinaman, what do you want me to say?" Other motifs came into her mind: instruments, tree trunks, dances, shouts, parts torn off. Blood on the ground, and an eternal human heat. This was on another, much older continent.

Catherine would have wanted to cry out in horror, but how, how was she to explain how the mechanism worked, and that so personal a horror, mingled with pleasure, came from the photograph of the Chinese man? How was she to explain that the horrible ecstasy of the Chinese man was one of her own states and was communicated to her soul from the inside toward the outside? "Get it out of my sight, I don't want any more, I don't want any more, I feel like throwing up." Yet the Chinese man who had thus come into her resembled Luc Pascal, but in the opposite direction.

MASSACRE OF THE INNOCENTS

"Noémi and I are in a rather sumptuous hotel room. There are many rugs, wall hangings. I am seated, undressed. At the same time I see myself from the back in the place where I am sitting undressed, and in addition Noémi, who is there, is also me with smaller proportions. So I see myself from the back and nude, and I am looking at my shoulder; I note that this shoulder, in the spot where they used to brand convicts, bears—I feel no shame in confessing it—a distinctive mark. The mark looks like a cauliflower; it's a wound with which I am marked, in the shape of a cauliflower, no doubt from a vile disease, maybe the wound from a cancer, the vilest disease I know. In fact it resembles—I've seen engravings—a cancer in cauliflower shape from a . . . you understand. I also remember that my father told me once a very long time ago: don't eat your cauliflower so fast, and that because he had said that to me, I cried bitter tears. . . . The wound on my shoulder is a red rectangle. I say, looking at the surface, that 'it's also like a cake,' and when I have said these words, someone comes in whom I can't make out because he is behind my back; but he comes in, he approaches; with instruments he extirpates the cake with the help of Noémi, and in an instant there appears a nice, clean little cut. But now it is moving into my arm! It is necessary to peel my arm because it is swollen and brown! M. Leuv. does nothing for my arm, and during this time my arm swells up. I have to tear the skin with my nails and pull at it, it hurts like the dickens there; finally the arm is done for; *fit only to be cut off.*

"And that's all for that business.

"I am lying in the same room next to Pierre Demini, and we are looking lovingly at each other. Our beds are twin beds. However, on Pierre's bed a very small woman is sitting. It's Gloria, that's her name, blond and sluttish like Venetian women, and I know her well in the world. For example, I can't figure out what she's up to. Probably she's only scratching her scalp under her mop of hair, as usual. Smaller than in reality, she represents what is old and ancient. I observe also that Gloria on the bed is adopting the poses of a bold woman, and consequently I understand that Pierredemini and she . . . Yet here is a new element, a considerable event. While I was looking at Gloria, the two beds were traversed by an aluminum bathtub, three-quarters full of water; and in the bathtub is the meat cut out from my father.

"At the same moment, of course, the funeral director appears: I recognize my friend Massa-Aaron, Gloria's husband. As always, he is very distinguished, very smart. Little Massa-Aaron approaches with reserve and sadness, wearing a monocle and an annoying smile under his mustache. Because I know that he is the *undertaker* (in English), he says to me in Jewish English: 'I have done my best; so sorry not to have been able to put *thine* really under. (Fact he is floating.) It was too expensive.'

"In fact, I think it would cost too much, as he says: the pieces must remain here. The bathtub with the pieces is sunk into the beds. If it moves at all, it isn't much. What a situation! The director looks with indulgent pity at the daughter of the dead man (me), who hasn't left her bed.

"I hear a rhythmic, intense, magnificent music. The themes that express vast ideas of an inexhaustible richness decompose further into a thousand little labyrinths of an extraordinary charm. 'The music is carving out the heavens,' it is filling the space exactly. The phrases, the songs, separate out, become pieces, bars, sticks that fall onto one another, that pile up, and with what modern science, with what primitive naïveté the sticks come and gather to form my pyre! I'm going to be burned in the town square. Traffic is stopped temporarily; they are waiting for my last breath. A man in black appears. I know him. I call him 'Pascal.' He cocks his revolver. He puts the barrel of the revolver against my temple. In an instant he blows my brains out! And they light the fire!

"Gloria!"

* * *

This story which Catherine told to Little X. did not seem to move her. "I see a lot of evidence," she said. The Little One reflected with extreme concentration; the muscles of her face could be seen to contract.

"The first story," she murmured, "is stupid, poorly designed, poorly done. So we have to start over again from the beginning, with the same ideas that are in your head. What do you think of the second one?"

"I see in it . . . *hatred* against all men. See, look, there's a man forcing us, putting a revolver to our temple! I'll call that one *allmen*. And then there's the other one, the distinguished 'undertaker,' who doesn't succeed, you understand, who can't manage anything, right? who leaves us in midstream. And there he is, the husband we love: he has a second woman on his bed. Aha! There they are, I tell you, there they are, all of them!"

"You're forgetting the main thing," the Little One answered gravely. "You have to start it all over. All right . . . I'm going to make a drawing for you.

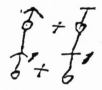

"Those are the people on the twin beds. The pointed one on the left is the father, the other one, who is flat, is the mother. But at the same time, below the father is Pierredemini, and below the mother is you; I'm identifying them by putting a sort of little *1* next to them. All right, let's begin:

wanted to have for herself

because she said: Why aren't we inseparable in a single entity? What can I do to be unseparated? She said this to him, but he didn't understand, didn't want the thing to be done. Anyway, she didn't know what thing. She wanted only to be mingled with him and for them to be mingled with her and for this never to be separated again. She couldn't stay like that any longer, her here and him there, so strong was her desire to belong to him, so strong her need no longer to be alone outside, but to melt. So she told him this, but he didn't want to understand. And she didn't dare think whether he was right or whether he was wrong, he was so much stronger and more handsome than she, he was so much larger; but unable to detach herself from her desire, she dreamed of joining him to her by some magical means, she didn't know what means, but to draw him into her, since she couldn't melt into him! And since she was appropriating things that were good and because this was the real way, by eating them, she began to dream that she was appropriating him by eating him. But probably because one can't really eat what is alive, or else because she was also very bad, she made him die and cut him up before she ate him. It was thus that for a long time she ate him in secret. No one knew anything about it. And because all this is very bad and forbidden—yes, forbidden, by the one who makes the law inside and who prevents bad actions—she felt hatred, and she also felt she was vile, she was guilty, and the more guilty she was, the more she felt hatred. That's the way it was. But she still dreamed that she was eating him with delight. That's the way it was. And she also had the feeling of not being loved anymore. Because if she was eating him after causing him to die, she had had her love, she did not have it anymore. (And also, because he had said to her: no.) This is not at all what the little one would have wanted. This was not the path she wanted to take, but she had no other! She felt that the main thing had been taken away from her, as though someone had cut it off from her. She felt at the same time that to be a girl is a misfortune, because one is not loved and because one does not have the means to impose love properly on someone else. And that's why, putting herself in the mother's place, she always sees the father she loves cut up. For our suffering, girls that we are, goes very far, and lasts a very long time! She told him this, but he didn't want to understand. One day Osiris the sun died; he was put into the Nile in pieces; now his wife, Isis, goes off looking for him at night; she finds him, and she puts the pieces back together again, she mends him. Osiris comes back to life. In this way, it's much more beautiful, and it's eternal. Then, seized with terror because everything she had once attempted in love was so bad, the woman lying there

knew that inevitably it would also be bad with

who came from outside and whom she loves once again, who is called Pierredemini. She was in despair! She felt that the situation with this one would be the same, and that she would want to kill him, since in his presence she found herself the same, amputated and diminished. She knew this would always repeat itself and that it was inevitable. So she was in despair. As in the story of Isis, she wanted this to end in a god, but it was also necessary for her to be punished, so she said, let me become divine by burning on a pyre, and she summoned a great deal of music to accompany her as she died. She wants to die nobly, divinely! If he did not want to understand—what she is doing is more beautiful, more eternal.

"You ask me what is this individual with the revolver who shoots the king's daughter when she is on the pyre. Well . . . this time I don't know anymore. So, I don't know what to say about him, about that one. See, this time I'm giving up!"

XII

As for her, during this time, she was not resisting the Mongol. Luc Pascal was settling into her life with greatest ease.

Who was this Mongol? She did try to find out, but not very hard, for she did not want to know too much about anything. The Mongol certainly had complete authority in what he was. Had she learned that he saw no one and lived in order to write in red notebooks, sitting up in his bed, preferably during the night, she would have said that she had guessed as much. But also, this man who had raised so many things to a high place, to a sublime place, was not the one who devoured Catherine's hand with kisses. When the Mongol emerged from his seclusion, he was a man like all the others, even more of a man than most. He then appeared tall, clean-shaven, dressed with care. He must also have had certain things to seek forgiveness for, because he maintained an odd silence on the subject of his past. One sensed in him a culpability, of which he made use, for he claimed that man owes something to original sin. And so it was that Catherine advanced wavering-ly toward acquaintance with the Mongol; she would not expect to have known him, anyway; she was captivated, frankly, by his mysterious authority. She found herself attracted to the Mongol's power; surprised by the changes in level that power presented; and stopped—held to him, finally, by something else.

She felt that other thing, then suddenly she no longer felt it. She felt it as the most curious thing in the Mongol, and that was why a voice said to her, about this: don't look in that direction. Yet it is particularly sweet to love someone in these circum-stances. The power of attraction increases exactly to the same degree as the feeling of prohibition.

What threw some light on the Mongol's secret was a story he told one day without preamble. The Mongol needed to tell this.

"The scene takes place in a mountain village in Italy. The heat of the afternoon is stifling above the majestic trees, and the lake gives off glints of a sword. A woman is sitting on the front doorstep, in the lane, with a crony. It is in vain that the village knows what is going to happen. The man, called Zeppe, is an old fellow of sixty-two. For the past week he has announced it to anyone who would listen. The day before, in town, he bought himself a knife six inches long and one and a half inches wide. Zeppe appears in the shop of the *prestinaio*—the baker—who also runs a café; it's a few steps from the lane. He takes off his shoes; he puts on espadrilles. Zeppe, in the lane, sees the woman: she tries to go back into her house, but Zeppe is already putting his arm around her neck; the crony runs off; all the men are in the fields. At the first thrust of the knife, which strikes at her heart but too high up, she cries out 'Mama!' Zeppe answers: 'Don't be afraid, you are in my arms,' and then eight thrusts of the knife, one of which goes all the way into her belly, the seven oth-ers around her heart. Her heart, her belly. Then he lets her fall. I should point out that killing a woman produces very little blood.

"The children come running from all directions to see. He drags her a little over the pebbles and wipes his knife on his pants. The woman had cried out, but not much, and her outcry had nothing tragic about it, it was as though she had slipped. The *curé*, hearing the children's howls from the church square where he lives, arrives with the choirboy; he sends for the sacraments; without concerning himself with the murderer, he goes and bends over the woman, but he is blessing a dead person, while Zeppe continues on his way, saying: 'I'm damned happy you're dead.' Having said this, the murderer goes down on his knees and pretends to kiss the earth. Zeppe, whom no one can touch, goes back up to the *prestinaio*. Putting down his knife, he declares: 'That's how you have to deal with women.' He wants to have a glass of wine; they refuse it to him."

Catherine said petulantly, "Who told you that horror story?"

"I witnessed it. I saw the whole thing."

"You were in the lane?"

"I was there."

"You didn't try . . . or were you afraid?"

"Neither one. It was a fine representation of ritual murder and hysteria. As I told you, the weather was splendid."

And the point where Catherine was enlightened as to the Mongol's tendencies was when she perceived the joy and pleasure with which one can narrate—and hear—a story of this sort. Beneath a superficial indignation she was pleased. And he had not described that abomination for nothing. Because he was even more satisfied than she was. Yet he, too, on the surface, said that the villagers had been relieved to see the man arrested, put in prison, no doubt for life. Thus Catherine and the Mongol were thinking the same way, and Catherine felt, from the state of her linen, that her body was not remaining indifferent.

Thus the Mongol could define himself as the *man who scared a woman*. Would he have wanted to kill her? True or false, all of this was in the Mongol. Catherine had no desire to meet a violent death, but she was very excited by the risk she had to run in order to approach this poet; and why hadn't the Mongol ever killed anyone? Could it be that he had punished himself in advance by putting himself in prison to write his poetry?

He said to Catherine with an air of imbuing a word with a double meaning, "Now I see that I was expected." Expected! She asked herself whether she should tolerate such boldness, or admire so acute an intuition. "To show the picture of my life," he said, "I would like to be able to use strong and repellent colors; but, alas, there is no way of interesting you, of *exciting* you with the customs of a solitary man. When one is exiled in oneself, one necessarily adopts reprehensible habits. One no longer thinks like the rest of the world, as they very clearly express it. For a very long time now, my mind has created its barriers toward the outside, and even in the inside. You will have to make the best of it," he added, "my dear friend."

"But also," said the woman's voice, "why should one have murdered life in that way?"

"When one's dissatisfaction is limitless," answered Luc Pascal, looking Catherine Crachat straight in the face, "the demands one makes are absolute."

* * *

Then she pursued her own thought: "But what are you claiming, sir, by insinuating that I exert a magical force, and that I am becoming attached to you? You know very well that I'm a true medusa: restless, I float on waters that have the cloudy and unpleasant color that I have myself. So that I wouldn't be able to say I like your skull covered in wrinkled white skin (for you keep it away from the sun under a soft felt hat), whose pallor makes one think through contrast that your fringe of dark hair attests to some somber malady. Your nose, too open to the wind, seems to be sniffing out unsavory things. The flesh your eyes are set in is not at all reassuring, it jars with their gaze. Your shoulders give an idea of your age, shoulders deformed by your sedentary profession. Even though I am no longer an elegant woman, in my view you dress badly, so awfully badly that one could not decently go out for a walk on your arm: just look at the shape of the collar riding up, of the deformed trouser legs that remind one of tubes, and those wrinkles about the crotch that I particularly detest the sight of. Certainly it is not *you* that I love: the thing would be, you agree, grotesque. But there may be qualities in you that I love. You are certainly noble, and of a sensitivity so rare that one forgets the ill-naturedness in which it pleases you to live. You are, in short, what they do indeed say, a poet; you are *detached* from everything that *holds* us: there it is, the diabolical force with which you fill your literature. I allow myself to admire you. If you are pernicious, you are strong, and since you are strong, you are beautiful.

"In sum, I love you."

Catherine confessed this thought neither to Pascal, nor to Little X., nor to anyone else. Love for the Mongol would lack a formal opening and would pass unnoticed. In fact, where was it occurring? In a person hidden inside Catherine; as for Catherine, what could it matter to her whether there was love or no love and whether the physical kiss was like this or like that. One knows about her indifference.

* * *

But she saw that nothing was escaping the private police. The Little One ran hither and yon declaring what she had seen. Monsieur Leuven listened behind a curtain, or put his head, previously made up, over the wall. Catherine did not care about the Little One, who wasn't listened to by anyone except M. Leuven, and since they both belonged to the cops, they could talk all they wanted! No, Catherine had only one worry, when she saw the affair developing, and that was that she would be seen by Noémi. Even though Noémi also had "something new in her life," as we shall see, she was still watching Catherine. Reticent, grotesque, and solemn, Noémi was waiting; or else she blinked her eyes as she looked at Catherine with an unsavory air, for no one rivaled Noémi in giving an impression of obscenity in her gaze. "Fool your friends!" mused Catherine. "But I know who you are. You are me, but worse." Yet Noémi had gentle manners, a distinguished bearing. "But I know who you are." "Lower than I, and stupider, you are the woman I was. With your own manner. You always live on the level of a point, and on the level of that little point where reality is not attained, you remain profoundly immobile. You reduce others to being seen from the point in question. And now, from that point, you would like to interest Trimegiste."

When Noémi listened to music she presented an expressive picture. "Mademoiselle Noémi," Trimegiste had already said, "is a fit subject for a painting when she listens to music." The more elevated the style of the music, the more successful Noémi's picture was. Her legs perfectly joined, her back straight, giving her a bosom, she seems, by her expression, to have fallen into a deep stupor! She is smiling. From a head heavy as a bowling ball, her gaze goes directly out to meet infinity.

Where Noémi is concerned, things really started there, if one considers them properly. Trimegiste, having seen the picture, wanted to see it again and *loved* seeing it again. From that moment on, we are involved in love. Noémi listening to music revealed an ideal creature; Trimegiste yearned to find the ideal creature again; and to arrive at that end, he loved Noémi. Then he installed her in superb seats at concerts and operas so that, keeping a little in the shadows, he could watch the play of her features. In this way he contrived to have his particular pleasures with Mademoiselle

Noémi without pushing things too much. But then the accident happened. (The story comes from Flore, who has it from Noémi.) They were in orchestra seats listening to *The Magic Flute* when, during the second act, Noémi became emotional and suddenly stood up. Once she was up, Noémi disturbed the audience all around her because she had to go out! The most serious part of it was that a very bad smell accompanied her! At the intermission Monsieur Trimegiste went looking for her in the hallways; from the bathroom, where she had taken refuge, Noémi had gone outside.

And there it was; that public indecency drew them together. The event had a decisive importance. Was it pity? Was it desire? In any case, now they are inseparable. He no longer makes a move without her, nor she without him. There are nothing but letters, telegrams, express-mail letters, telephone calls. Georgette was promptly eliminated. Trimegiste now spends all his time conquering Noémi; if he knew enough not to hurry, he would have Noémi's "yum-yum," he would bring about the fall of an angel. They did the thing with money first, so to speak, since Trimegiste was gambling Noémi's little fortune on the stock exchange. Noémi, who did not even have enough left to buy a shirt for herself and who allowed herself to be supported by M. Trimegiste both in luxuries and in necessities, was happy, truly happy, when she imagined that, whatever happened, her fortune was in M. Trimegiste's hands, and it hardly mattered whether he earned money from it or gave it to someone else, as long as he enjoyed it.

XIII

THE MARVELOUS GREEKS

"I have seen such terrible things, my beloved, that I take pleasure in seeing you. You are handsome, in fact. You are severe and you are amiable. You are young and you are old. I notice that you have many faces that glide over one another, and it changes all the time; but as it thickens, it's you.

"In profile you are a Chinese. You know, a Chinese motionless in a temple, what they call, I think, a bonze: he sometimes eats rice, without ever bending his torso, and he speaks without blinking his eyes, and he laughs without moving his wrinkles. Actually you would more likely be a warrior: I suppose there is a terrible force in you, abnormal, an annihilating force; it's your Chinese warrior profile; a habit of suffering with joy, that's your Chinese bonze profile again; and you torture according to principles, and you're going to torture me—but oh surprise!—these Chinese things disappear by magic and give place to a very young kid.

"You must be superb when . . . Forgive me that indiscretion. I won't do it again. I'll never think of you again in that way. It's very bad. Of course you read my thoughts, because you have a sorcerer's knowledge of the same nature as your strength, corrosive and ravaging. I'm very much afraid of you. But then you are a man; that excuses many things of one sort and another. I will have the courage to repeat that I would like to know how you are a man. Oh, you are terribly occupied with me and you will be my happiness, and I have been thinking of nothing but you for several days. But it isn't that clear thing that I want to say. I am talking to you, do you understand me?

"You are not a Trimegiste. You do not wrap a woman in lots of threads like a spider. No, you're the attacking sort, that's what you are. One can let oneself go when you appear. You risk the whole game in order to have the whole animal. I could really murder you, you know? Women sometimes get out of it that way. And sometimes it's the men who murder. Nastasia Philippovna must be murdered quite necessarily, she can't avoid it; and if it wasn't Rogozhin who dealt the blow, it would be the Idiot himself.

"But these extreme solutions are not pleasant.

"You make me think of nature. I see the mountains again, loaded with enormous bunches of leaves, boom, boom, one on top of another, in the sky. And how about it, have you lost your childhood enough yet, huh? Yet, inside your eyes I see a spring: it comes, no one knows from where, but it crops up, and it tries to dampen the desert! But I will make your natural springs spurt up all right! I assure you that I'm good. Do you believe me? I'm very good. I only want to be happy with you in nature, in the day, under the sky; I want to love you the way I like it, in the wilderness, I want to put myself there with a man like you. You have to let me do as I like. You mustn't intimidate me, because you are much stronger, and at my age . . . I don't accept your civilized and moral arguments. I want a big Arabian baboon and you can very well be it. Why wouldn't you? That's the meaning of your beauty. I need real things, you understand? I've spent the entire first part of my life in mistakes and misunderstandings, I've always taken someone for someone else. Now I want to take someone for himself, and I will wait to see how he behaves and what he can do, and I want him to take me for what I am and what I can do, and by this path we will no doubt arrive at the immense, immense 'pleasure in nature.'

"You who live in isolation and as an artist, give me the desire to be the universal woman: for example, you make me think of the Greek statues. I would do *Venus Anadyomen* very well for you. I would have dark skin the color of a coconut, and warm drops falling from my eyes, sliding over my oily parts. The base of my spine would be sparkling like the sun in the triangle of the three dimples, and the wind would roll my polished hair over my shoulders. My front would be smooth and rough (as is befitting to Venus), a column protected by my pelt. My face would be inanimate as it emerges from the waters of the sea. Birth in seawater, seawater of birth. I would also play the secondary subjects for you: that of the naiad, that of the trumpet shell, that of the seahorse. Because my body is able to represent all things. My love contains all the roles that please your desire. You may prefer to see me merely white and passive: *Europa* abducted by the bull, ravished by Jupiter, always in the waves of the sea. This reminds me of a museum picture I saw when I was a child, and it exerted such a fascination on me that as I saw it, I sweated with love. Look. The bull is white, majestic, Olympian. Europa is of another whiteness, and her pubis is cream; the ocean is green and moves under her toes. No; you're getting tired of this; you don't like it. Then I'll go down under the earth and into Hell and I will be *Hecate*. Pale, magical incarnation of the moon—when, in her third quarter, she rises with a false aspect, spreading like some spittle over the middle of the sky where a storm is breeding—I make my way to the underworld which contains the souls of the dead as they wait; here I will be used for enchantments, ransoms, and, close to Persephone, I hand down my implacable decisions. Have great fear of me, of my cold, irritating beauty, and above all of my smile, which was the ancient upturning of Diana's lips. What could be fiercer than *Diana?* She is beautiful, she is healthy, her hymen has not been forced, she cuts off the members of animals, her smell is the most potent in the perfumed forests and it's her own odor that she kills! But Hecate is more mysterious: for I do not hunt, and I kill. This half-godly creature that I have actually been seems to me to be the one that is best suited to the atrocious accent of your beauty. Oh, as for you, you know that 'in the depths dwells the angry old god about whom, assuredly, it is best to say nothing.'

"But you, oh demon, will also demand a human character!

"After Venus's flank clad in vapors and her intoxicating tuft, which turn our hearts in confusion, how sweet are the shoulders of young *Ariadne* covered by an overlarge peplos, with a body like unto a stream! She is a true, plump virgin finding her way through the labyrinth of deadly box trees, of poisoned springs, each turn of which must herald the sudden irruption of the Monster, and where, under a low ceiling, you pant. Ariadne holds you; her face is grave, and she is dressed in white. Her thread catches on the little outcroppings of the terrain, and she actively strains her ears while her mouth murmurs, 'I'm here! I'm here!' She will extricate you from this evil pass, profound and ancient, where you have been forever caught, terrified, blocked, frozen before the threat of ignominious death and steeling yourself to meet it. What have I wanted, with my sloping white shoulders: your confidence only. Grant it to me; promise me marriage; then, brought back out into the open air, before the splendid cloudy sky, you will lie with my sister.

"Let us go on a journey. I shall be your mother, your sister, your little girl, your whore. I shall be your toy, your confessor. Your muse, your angel. I shall be your ordained demon. I shall be your warrior in linen armored and girdled. I shall be your holy woman, in black. I shall be the cloak, I shall be the washer of crockeries, I shall be the protector of intelligence, I shall be the woman murdered in the village. I shall be the boy, if you like. For in your love, one must be, enormously and a great deal, one sex and the other, one world and the other, one and many, one must give oneself much trouble before exhausting all that nature has accorded us!"

XIV

BALLOONS

During the twenty days of a trip that she took with him, "it" occurred several times, and "the marvelous Greeks" tried to incarnate themselves in all sorts of ways. She could say that she had a great deal of talent. Nor indeed was he behindhand in invention and courtesy. In one or two circumstances, because aroused bodies project light around them, she had been able to declare to Luc Pascal, "I love you very much," and then, with the help of the marvelous Greeks, she had felt completely calm. It was therefore necessary that the marvelous function; without the marvelous, she was afraid of being cold. If she saw herself being cold one single time, it would be all over. The "marvelous" was a game she had imagined, as though she had been able, by means of beauty, to form herself into a "superior body" that would itself do the thing easily and through which she could be happy. Yes, but "is it really me?" she asked herself; and she wasn't at all sure of it. With the "marvelous Greeks," it wasn't enough to obtain a little happiness, a happiness that still had the flavor, the character, of "marvelous Greek"; it was necessary after that to act effectively upon others and win successes afield. A very distinct feeling said to her that between this and all of reality there was an unbridgeable distance.

After she had developed considerably her skills in the marvelous, concordantly with him, Catherine felt that nothing had been achieved, for the Mongol was not alive in her and she was not alive in the Mongol. Thus did she continue to name him to herself: Mongol, which proved that she took him for a masculine form and not for *her* man. It was possible that the Mongol was happy; why yes, the way she was. Of such happiness one cleanses onself when the kiss is ended; nothing is left. What had happened, what was there that had been changed? He remained dry, hard, and secretive about his earlier life; she had no influence over him; he had merely said, in order to awaken Catherine's jealousy, that he had been married to a superb woman and abandoned by her. For the Mongol, Catherine, as a very mysterious person, did not exist. Did he care about the extraordinary adventure in which she was involved; did he wonder why, for the past twenty-five days, she had not been going to see Leuven? Was he concerned, worried about her? So she said to herself: "Hence, nothing real and profound exists between us. The profound thing is not being touched—in any case, not in me, apparently." Sorry, but love with Pascal could have taken on a meaning, an immediate and profound meaning. She knew that. The story about the woman murdered by Zeppe, which he had told her very early on, and several other times, affecting her very strongly, arousing in her a very particular emotion . . . "Had I wanted anything like that role . . . love . . . yes, love with him . . . "

"But what about those fantasies, the marvelous Greek figures I had in my head?" They were balloons, balloons. Like balloons they swelled up, they grew out of all proportion and they were going to burst—to such an extent did they combine beauty and grotesqueness, and confuse everything, glory and absurdity. Balloons! She had believed in balloons! She had loved balloons. Well, she was going to have to go back to the real source, the truth, the modest truth, what was said at Monsieur Leuven's and with the Little One; yes, she was going to have to submit to it once again!

To live narrowly between those two . . .

* * *

Dr. Leuven, with his crude perspicacity and his *inanimate* nature, speaks and acts on a second level that she knows well. Get off at the second level, go through Leuven's door, and the famous person whom he was addressing no longer exists, one doesn't remember her.

Here one may be disoriented, distressed; one is never *mixed*. One knows just what to expect: next to you, the truth forges ahead, and the steps it takes are not yours. Leuven as human relation does not count. Of course, Catherine's relations with everybody else were souring in an unpleasant way; that's how one always behaves; one doesn't like the spectacle of love; one drives people away; for instance, with Flore there were scenes in which all sorts of nasty things came out that one had never suspected, like hairy animals! But Monsieur Leuven does not count. With this confessor one declares that one has taken a lover, that one has found pleasure in it, but immediately the event becomes more serious and, so to speak, loses its underlying color, its human content lowers. Moreover, it is useless to try to make M. Leuven jealous by brandishing this piece of news: he lacks the feeling that ought to respond to provocation. One mustn't hide from oneself the fact that, on the second level, M. Leuven's authority and forcefulness are formidable in the battle he has engaged, during which he strikes no blow; but is it a battle? Rather, it's the operation of capturing a very vicious conger eel deep under water. How we have descended, this time, from place to place: here we are far (we think) from fantasies and balloons.

* * *

When the Little One was quite assured that the new attachment had taken place, and was holding well, she made a sensational appearance.

Catherine suddenly saw the Little One, even littler. She came, she was visible against the black of the night. A pink little girl, old-fashioned, extraordinarily gay. Her blond hair, all curly, lifted around her head, stirred and undulated: they were out in the open air. Her furbelows were pink, her mitts were black, her little socks white, and besides that she wore a large black bow in the back.

How brilliant she appeared!

Sitting in the hay.

Catherine was applying herself to finding some gentle words for the dear little brilliant girl . . . when the scene changed completely. Rue Saint-Honoré, opposite the Crédit du Nord, the bank where Catherine has her savings account; traffic is blocked as a result of the presence of a hay cart on two wheels, filled with hay, on the same scale as the little girl—that is, very small—and it, too, is painted in striking colors. *The importance* of the hay cart is enormous, because it has stopped in front of the bank; because of it, once again, the traffic has become impossible, the cars are honking furiously, policemen are blowing their whistles, a crowd is gathering, and people are even coming to the windows of houses. Who's the owner of the hay cart, for God's sake! Whose is it? This hay cart, whose?

Just after, Catherine felt deeply preoccupied by the question of money. At Leuven's she would have to spend a lot and for a long time. Twelve hundred francs a week. Twenty weeks already. Twenty-four thousand francs. She had to count on other expenses coming to at least the same amount. Maybe to twice as much. Seventy-two thousand francs. Enough to buy a car again, since she had sold hers. The price of several furs and of ten dresses. Half her income! Catherine was not rich. Now this income was going down, inasmuch as (1) Flore had made some blunders in her investments; (2) everyone was losing hand over fist these days; (3) Catherine was not working, therefore no money was coming in, nothing on the horizon. (To complete the picture, wasn't it necessary to add: Luc Pascal is poorer still, he hasn't a thing to his name.) But if this business were to last two years . . . one hundred and fifteen thousand francs! She had heard of a Russian who had been paying for four or six years what she was paying. Suffering is nothing; but money! When one no longer has a job, one can no longer give out one's money, one must defend it penny by penny. Now, here was M. Leuven claiming that once the operation was finished, she would find herself with an increased capacity for activity, and consequently would earn money, more money than in the past. Don't give me that stuff!

Who was there to guarantee that the reasoning was disinterested? Besides, money is so dirty, so sh—ty; and say what you will, there is only one way of having money, the sh—ty way; money is money: "A rich man is one who has twice as much as you," says Trimegiste. From top to bottom it's the same passion of finding some at the expense of someone else. At the expense of someone else—at one's own expense—at the expense of life! To possess it is to be hanging onto a treasure that must necessarily disappear. Ah! Horrible formula, when one thinks about it: *I don't owe you anything more*. Prostitution is far preferable as a way of earning one's bread! . . . "Poor. I have a love of what is poor. I have a love of the Poor Man who has become like unto the lilies of the field. How it smites the heart when we come upon Holy Poverty. But what to do, what to do? Who, today, in this world, can be poor? The saints' greatest idea is banished from the world, it has been suppressed as useless. I wanted to practice poverty. I never succeeded. When I was poor I was worth nothing, and as soon as I had a value, money came to me the way it comes to everyone. At present I *want* to become poor. 'The lilies of the fields that toil not, neither do they spin.' But what to do, what to do? No matter. A great light is beside me in my life and . . . "

She did not question the idea that she should *separate herself* from all the people surrounding her. They had all worn thin and now their effect was to paralyze her in her heart. "He and I are going to get on a boat, leave, and the others will never see us again"—this was one of the reveries into which she would plunge (but just as she knew she would never be poor, she saw clearly that she would keep those people and live among them).

She retreated fiercely into herself. She experienced great interest in hearing the noises of her body. Inside her, there were noises, rumblings, borborygmi, which seemed significant to her, happy and reassuring, like the words of a private language whose meaning she had once known and which she had forgotten—not quite completely. Yes, this language expressed how, by certain movements of her substance, she belonged intimately to herself. Borborygmi were a body's song, its underlying spirit, and since they were her borborygmi, the primordial spirit of her body, she could at last take refuge there, with pleasure.

And one time she found that her belly was heavy! She was convinced that in her intestine must be the dead child that had so preoccupied her as a little girl. Then she felt a pain at a precise spot. Finally the idea and the sensation became so painful that she was examined; of course there was nothing there. She was frightfully disappointed. From disappointment, she slipped into a fury. Fury against herself, against life, against all she had been made to undergo.

"But you were so happy deep inside me, within me?"—"I can't talk anymore. It has to do with something else. *It* does not belong to your operation. *It*—is everything. And *it* is not strong enough! Otherwise I wouldn't be here! I wouldn't be here!"

A dismal depression set in and she went back to crying.

XV

THE SEARCH FOR THE AGGRESSOR

The sound of her voice became bizarre and intolerable.

She whimpered. She had to repeat a phrase three times in order to succeed in steadying her voice. She attributed this falseness of her voice to her sore throat, but she did not have a sore throat. One could distinguish two things, the weakness of her voice and the whimpering. It was the whimpering that bothered her most. The whimpering: the whining tone of a person put in the corner, who must confess a serious fault. And always when it was necessary to speak, to impose herself, the false voice won out.

This voice was so stupid that Catherine fell into confusion because of it. Truly the voice of an idiotic little girl. This exposed her to people's mockery. Luc Pascal pretended not to notice anything, out of malice. But others remarked: "What a strange voice! What a voice!"

"Just don't bother me," she retorted. "It's my throat."

The voice became even more peevish. How unhappy and irritated Catherine was! A new machination. . . . Noteworthy thing: since she had begun to talk in this way, Little X. had not shown herself.

One day when leaving Leuven, impossible to find the natural tone in which to say good-bye to him! *She doesn't know how to go away, how to say good-bye.* Then she took the tram that leaves from Etoile. She was supposed to meet the Mongol on the Left Bank.

In the full tram, she finds herself stuck in first class. Her eyes wander worriedly despite herself. She becomes aware of the fact that she is expecting to encounter an object and that her expectation is accompanied by fear. The people sitting down are conventional, bourgeois men who have the Legion of Honor, young girls who are going to their piano lessons. But, how is it that she didn't see right away that the seat opposite her is occupied—by a wagoner? The wagoner has his whip between his legs.

During the time of wondering, "How does it happen that one sees a carter with a whip in first class?" the scene is illuminated from within. Everything becomes different. A dazzling truth emerges, at the very moment when an extraordinary wave of emotion rises from her feet to her throat. She looks, she looks at the wagoner, and *she recognizes him.*

She has seen him before. It's him. Who does she mean—him? *Him.* It's obviously him. She has it. She's going to understand how it could be that it is him. They're going to have it out, at last, it's absolutely necessary. (Catherine's legs are trembling, she's sweating down her back.) The carter is a broad-shouldered man, blond, and he is looking at the floor; leaning forward, he has his two arms crossed and resting on his thighs. He is not moving at all. He seems completely inert. Perhaps he is not alive? But when one bends a little to try to see him, one makes out that the person has blue eyes.

I told you that he is not moving at all. Not even to breathe. Catherine intensely wants to exchange a word with the carter. By what indirect means can she make contact with him? In what manner can one address a carter in the tram, and talk to a statue? In the midst of all this, here is the place where Catherine *must* get out. She clings to the partition separating the compartments. *She cannot leave him.* She doesn't want to lose him. She must at least have the proof—the proof!—that this isn't an . . . illusion; and (to be certain) she touches him as she goes by, at the level of his knee. He is a man of flesh and blood.

She stifles a small cry. She has seen him again and touched him!

Outside, a confused mass of automobiles and trams arriving side by side, from many directions, because of the crossroads at this station, and a tempest of horns and sirens rises, while lights swirl on the wet pavement. She fled past one string of tram cars; she wiped at a splash of water from a wheel, then found herself in front of another tram. What was happening? Everyone was shouting, and especially a tram conductor, while pointing at her, so that she realized the shouts were for her and because of her. She had just enough time to pivot and turn sideways. Her body was caught between the sides of two trams moving in opposite directions, with a heavy clanking noise; the forward one grazed her under the breast and tore away from her the fur she was wearing on her shoulder.

. . . When she understood that she had wanted to be crushed (crushed by the wagoner's tram), tears filled her eyes. She was on the sidewalk; after a violent trembling, she knew that she would now have to "search." *Who* was the wagoner? Or rather, *whom* did the wagoner resemble? The wagoner recalled whom? Without transition, the figure of Debonnard, the doctor, appeared. Same shape body, same features, same blue eyes. Dr. Debonnard was the portrait of the wagoner. He was a doctor who had taken care of her at the time of Pierre, and several times since. She wanted to go and see Debonnard right away.

While she is hesitating, the memory changes. Here she is six months earlier, before a bookstore window, with Flore. She has already resolved inside herself to have herself operated on at Leuven's, but the operation hasn't begun. With Flore she is looking at the books that have just come out. Flore moves a short distance away at this moment and Catherine is approached by a blond, square-shouldered gentleman with blue eyes. (It is, in fact, Debonnard.) They chat familiarly; actually, Catherine likes Dr. Debonnard very much. But here is Flore, left out, though she would certainly like to enter the conversation. "I remember that I didn't want to introduce her. I blocked her path as much as I could." Catherine's memory became even clearer. "At the same time I felt myself blush right to the roots of my hair. When Debonnard left, she asked me resentfully who that gentleman might be. And she pointed out that I was red, red, like a peony. 'That was Dr. Bertrand,' I answered her. 'You don't know him.' I concealed the name from Flore. I lied to Flore immediately.

"I couldn't understand why I was lying to Flore . . . I'm going to understand why . . . The . . . the name. The name of the *shepherd,* of the carter. L . . . Me . . . Let's start over again, patiently. So at the moment when I met Debonnard who looks like . . . Listen . . . At that moment . . . Let's remain calm; I'm on the sidewalk, nothing more can happen to me and I'm not going to go to the Mongol's place. At the moment when I met Debonnard, at the moment when I met Debonnard, Debonnard, Debonnard. *Louis!* His name was Louis. But . . . the dream of the carter Louis.

The carter who said: 'Well, come close, little slip of a girl! Come close, come close now . . . '; who was holding a shovel . . . standing on the cart . . . a furious carter . . . He was swaying and turning the shovel over, a shovel full of muck, and the muck fell on me, I was covered with muck . . . " The dream was after meeting Debonnard.

Louis Moutier!

"I have his name. Louis. With him I was always going here and there 'on the farm.' I see him! In his hay cart, his sand cart. Here are the buildings and the manure pool. He had been a farmhand since he was 'just a kid.' Big strong boy. Hot-blooded, blond. I was three years old, one, two, or four? My father died when I was five and I left the farm immediately after. But I saw him again, I'm thinking about it, I saw him again, later. I must have been twenty: it was certainly the same face, but he was going gray. The guy on the tram was him still young, and Debonnard was him old. I remember. And that I behaved like a thorough guttersnipe: always in the filth, in water, under the bellies of the animals. That they had to shave my head because I was so dirty. I ate from a tin plate sitting on the doorstep with the hired men . . . no one on earth could have made me go into the dining room . . . But when my father was there I went into the dining room.

"There's the hayloft again.

"It's high, it's immense, and always full of sun. Nothing but field mice! The amount of hay there is! One gets lost in it. What a beautiful view! One sees a window with a rope for falling into the courtyard. One sees little animals on the floor and coming out of the walls. A slice of bread and butter is eaten in the loft. Louis is the king of the loft; one sees him wherever you look. *Quite a fellow, that Louis.* The lock. The lock to the hayloft. It is made of brass, with a key; I put the key in, I take it out; in the keyhole: Louis. Don't know how that can be. It's not me . . . Wait, another lock, I see another one. Where? In the apartment

belonging to . . . no, not in Paris . . . in the Château d'Estiévand
. . . maybe two years later? The lock to the bedroom where I have
shut myself up 'to sleep during the afternoon' and where I was
sleeping so deeply that they had to have the door forced by a
locksmith; how they scolded me that day, how they scolded me.

"My father.

"I see him clearly. He arrives on the threshold. He is good
with everyone. Everybody brings his illness to Monsieur the
Doctor. He kisses me. He says to me, 'Scullion.' Oh, how I feel
him, how I feel him! I see him so well and so distinctly. I think
he's going to speak. I had never seen him again like this. Oh
father, father! No woman had a father to compare to mine. They
said quite rightly that he had a good-natured look, serious and
tender; a fringe of beard around his neck. His nose was pinched
toward the bottom by two wrinkles. His mouth was lovely and
red; a softer, violet-tinged flesh ringed his eyes under thick eyelids. He looked like Our Lord . . .

"Poor father, his hair floats on the sides, artist-style. He puts
on top of it a not very clean felt hat, which he shoves back toward
the nape of his neck. His overcoat goes up in the other direction
and touches the hat. Oh dear man, oh poor dear man. He moist-
ens his finger to turn the pages of a book. How wonderfully well
he tells stories, for instance, as he watches the sparks coming out
of the logs and the little blue flames pursuing their lives in their
own way in the fireplace! Father is not Our Lord; rather, he's an
artist. He has a large black ring on his index finger. Father is
intelligent, he is knowledgeable, he knows how people live and
die, but he also knows that he himself is powerless, like a child.
So if he resembles Christ, one can say that it's an imitation."

Immediately after these details came a more complete image.
Again Catherine sees the Father, who, one Sunday afternoon, is
walking slowly behind the garden hedge, in the village. The path
slopes. The father is alone because it is Sunday. Does he think no

one sees him? The father is looking at the path. But Catherine's little eye passes through the leaves. Oh, it's another father. Is he perhaps already dead, this father, that he has assumed so sad and so severe a mask? How full of darkness is his gaze; one doesn't know whether it's because of fear or because of an unknown feeling; how full of darkness his gaze is when he stares at the rising path in front of him. It is true that he is not walking very straight, despite the beautiful day. But he keeps mopping his forehead. He has dampened a whole handkerchief with his sweat. He can't take it anymore. The loving eye through the hedge gazes fondly at the father tottering along and registers the smallest motions of the Father when he sits down on a tree trunk.

* * *

She was just thinking of these profound images—the loft, the lock—which were flying around her like butterflies, when she fell asleep. And a large pink baby lay on the grass of the meadow. The large pink baby, perfectly familiar to her, was full of the joy of living: the baby rolled around on the grass and played and enjoyed the greatest possible pleasure. Behind, there was a black figure whom one couldn't see and who was called "my father."

Catherine was approaching an extremely serious matter.

She scarcely had time to reflect on the precipitous events. The extremely serious matter was becoming clear or was withdrawing into hiding. The extremely serious thing—or the crime—wanted to come to light. Catherine, in her searching, pushed the thing away and removed it to a distance. There was the crime, the author of the crime, and lastly the reality of the crime. Suddenly Catherine believed she was strong enough to confess something to Police Inspector Leuven—no, nothing more precise: "I liked showing myself."

"Nothing more precise," he rejoined. "Let's try to move on."

"The lock."

"Yes, the lock!"

"*Someone* locked it, or did I lock it?" Yet she still said: "Don't know." And abruptly: "It's funny. Why did the name Moutier come back just before the loft and the lock?" And she answered Inspector Leuven, who was not questioning her anymore: "Because he was the one who took me to the hayloft."

The large Jew asked her, "He *took you to the hayloft?*"

"It's possible. But what I mean is that I remember how Madame d'Estiévand was furious because one afternoon I fell deeply asleep behind a door that had a lock, and that I had locked it. The lock was made of brass, I see it clearly, large and shiny. That caused quite a stir! I didn't want to wake up, they had to force the door." Then Catherine said without hesitating: "The second time I closed the door in order to recall the first time better. The first time, he was the one who closed it."

"He was the one who locked you in?"

"The carter." Yes, but then the Father arrives by another route.

"Can you say that your father came to the hayloft?"

"Oh never! He detested Louis!"

"So you didn't go to the hayloft when your father was there?"

"On Sundays, no."

"But on Saturdays?"

"Oh, yes."

"You didn't go to the hayloft when your father was at the farm on Saturdays?"

"Never!"

The inspector said with a certain severity: "I conclude from this that there were days when you could go to the hayloft with pleasure, and other days when it was very bad to go there."

"But look, that happened in the year when my father died!" And because she had mentioned the death of her father, everything was covered with a black sheet, she fell silent.

Later she sees herself lying down once again; but it is she, it's not the pink baby any longer, it's really she in the darkness. Like the first time, she knows there is someone there, someone invisible. What is he doing? This is what he's doing: he's putting out her eyes. He seizes a large nail and with a single large nail he does the job: he plunges it in, through both eyes. This cruel act causes paralysis, but she is very happy to be paralyzed. Thus the punishment will have no end, nor her pleasure either, nor her horror either, so that she will always have her pleasure, her horror, and her punishment.

The interrogation began again. "We have understood. And you want this never to end, despite the shame of being blind."

"Despite!" Catherine suddenly lowered her tone. "Ah—I feel it now." She remained silent for a long while and said again, "I feel it."

"You feel it."

"Louis Moutier."

Catherine threw her head into her arms to cry over what was. She stood up and went back home.

XVI

FATHER FORBIDDEN

However, once again (as soon as she closed her eyes) the father passed behind the hedge with the guilty look of a transgressor, with a painful quality of the forbidden. Was he a transgressor because she had transgressed a sacred commandment by loving him in a certain way, or because he had transgressed the commandment on his part? Was he therefore forbidden because they had done something bad? Or because she had dreamed of it? Or forbidden for another reason? He had, it seemed, he had to be for a reason infinitely vaster and with an irreparable effect. It was in this sense that she believed she "did not have a right to the Father," and it was then that she trembled from head to toe,

because this reality was much more horrible to consider, to rediscover, to reexperience, than the other that had appeared first and
with gradually more consistency (a farmhand named Louis had
apparently taken her to the hayloft and there, several times, had
used her in the hay).

What did the Father want? "How to appease your departed
ones." "How to find peace again with you, for the peace is disturbed." "How to be your daughter." At this moment Little X.
emerged unexpectedly from behind a curtain, greeted Catherine
politely, and put her index finger on her forehead. "I know everything," she said. She continued in these terms: "I know what is
happening, not only having to do with Louis, but with the Other;
before, during and after."

"Oh, speak, speak!" Catherine wanted to say. But not a word
came out of her throat.

STORY OF VAGADU

"Refresh your memory!

"What was half-light, half-dark, and caressed in secret, and
neither seen nor known in another place, encountered the truth,
brutal and exterior. The impact echoed, and we can still hear it.
Then love fell back, wounded, returned to its origin or hid itself;
and the soul of love, *with death inside,* having gone off to hide
itself far away, was called Vagadu.

"But everything that was experienced remains."

After that solemn preamble, Little X. gave the explanations.

"The little five-year-old girl loved the Father. As a woman, she
yearned to receive the love of the Father and dreamed of possess-
ing the Father as man, entirely for herself, for always. She wanted
to attract the Father closer, even closer to her breast, she wanted
to pass into him while he passed into her, the way a woman and

a man do. We have seen a gloomy story that had taken place earlier, according to which she had wanted to devour him and in that way had almost lost him. At the present hour, she had turned in another direction, and as soon as she would see her father she would experience an enchanting pleasure. She breathed only for him, and all week she would wait for Saturday, which was her father's day. What her father said and did were expressly for her; if by chance he looked at the least thing besides her, she itched with the desire to tear the thing to pieces. And all the people around her father could have died through her fault, because with respect to each of them she had thought a thousand times: I will kill you! Well, she did not lose one opportunity to display herself to the father with her pretty manners, in her nature, in one way or another, and in this she was very cunning; she took care that it should be understood in her father by the one who could understand. And soon she was thinking only of that, and how that was progressing, between her father and her, and what new inventions she would find to take possession of her father's heart. Yet now anger came. The Father was not paying enough attention. The Father hardly looked at the little girl's tricks and was not surprised by her inventions. The Father did not even scold her. The Father did not think about love because he was too weak. The Father was too weak because he was treating his illness. Oh yes, we were very irritated with the father who had no strength, and we watched with anger as our relations with him degenerated. We had reached the height of our anger, of our anger and our love, when . . . the Father disappeared, there was no more father.

"The Father was dead.

"It was because of the anger. Vagadu came right away. Vagadu looked at him, lying on the bed with the earth-colored face of the Great Judge, in the midst of the flowers; Vagadu arrived and said: 'That's certainly what it is. His yellow face is my face!' And she ran off shouting: 'Who killed the Father? It was you.'

"Vagadu went on to say: 'Since I killed him and it was my fault that he died, it is therefore my fault that my love died and it is impossible that it can be otherwise.' And we answered: 'The Father is forbidden to us; we do not have the right to have a father.' In the end the sorrow lasted a long time. And if there was something that was not in the cemetery, and that tried to grow back . . . "

Catherine, until then deeply prostrated, murmured in her turn: "And would it be in that accursed year that the farmhand Louis approached us from behind? We weren't able to say whether it was nasty or pleasant, but we thought: That man can certainly poke my eye out, I will be paralyzed; and that way I'll have my punishment, which is continuing, and my pleasure along with it, which is continuing."

The Little One resumed her speech where she had left off.

" . . . If there was something that wasn't in the cemetery, and that tried to grow back, it was the love you and I had for each other, which prevented our falling completely into Vagadu! However, in the midst of all those great misfortunes, one small path still opened up, the path toward heaven. The person living in her sorrows kept thinking about the father she had had. And so it happened that the father grew, grew, the way one can grow when one no longer has a body, and assumed new clothing. It was her fault the Father had died, and it was forbidden to her to have a father, thus the Father was now of the pure substance of heaven. If one said that he had been otherwise before, one was lying. He had never been more than an Image. And then, truly, the little girl began to console herself a little with this Father who was immense like the sky and who, because he had suffered so much, was Christ. Yes, our father died by our fault and Christ is in the grave by our fault and to redeem us all."

This was the way the little girl sensed the Father in her very pure moments; and her father was Christ in the grave. The little girl was also, in this affair, Christ in the grave.

"This is why, Catherine, we, the other ones, *haven't had life, only death.*

"Do you recall that you were forced to open the body of the large Christ to look inside? Ah, today you understand. You opened whose body? Christ's, because you must go and see what happened in the mystery of your five-year-old heart. And what did Christ become, when the cloth over his face slipped? A rather stupid dead man: the father.

"There, it's finished."

"You're wrong," said Catherine.

XVII

The injunction *Thou shalt!* is the oldest. The injunction *Thou shalt!*—which changes into *It is forbidden to!*—is a somber police-man whose clothes are as stiff as metal tubing, stretched tight as drumheads, and with a visage that is round, congested, expressionless. At the time the person took form, the flooding forth of things had already halted and the instinct of death had been set in motion. The latter did indeed require a forceful agent to ensure its predominance, against the soft-singing siren of pleasant life, withal impure and sinful.

The imperative policeman, deaf to what is not his duty, nails you in flagrante delicto because of these desires and these needs that you have. The policeman is in connivance with them: for without them, what would there be for him to do? The police-man is in charge of the establishment of *fault:* "What were you doing with your ten fingers? I saw you. What blasphemy were you uttering between your teeth? I heard you. What subversive thoughts were you harboring in your head? Let us apply the law of correction." This devil is in the service of the law. Now the law has a bone to pick with nature: there is an abomination hidden in this nature, which must be repressed; one cannot doubt that in the depths of the state of nature there dwells a fault that is one with *existence;* we have no other means of obtaining improvement and order than to destroy a little of that evil nature!

It is this policeman with his round limbs who did all the damage.

He probably struck an ill-aimed blow. Little Catherine's terror has fastened onto him and originates from him. This agent of order must be the wrongdoer; he is not sensitive to the case in point, he is stubborn in his views, and very unintelligent besides. One can even suppose that in his maneuver he (having some friends who are provocateurs) made use of that poorly identified character Louis, the farmhand. To what extent did the farmhand act? How did the child present herself in the circumstances? So many mysteries that we shall not clear up. Who knows whether this Louis Moutier, when he assumes the aspect of a criminal, is not quite simply a part of the Father, and in some sense his second side? Before the threatening policeman, the imagination, losing all touch with reality, may have cut the Father in two, the first half elevated all the way to heaven, and the second disguised as an ignoble carter who comes forward in order to abuse a little girl. But the facts are the facts.

* * *

Having reached the point where she was, Catherine realized that the events of her life had no objective existence, so to speak.

They had none because (their external reality being all that one would wish) their internal reality, their necessity, came from a point that was always the same—since they repeated the attitudes of a scene involving two or three figures that had formed once *for her,* a scene that constantly called for replaying in every way. One could say that the scene impregnated the objects that arose subsequently. The figures of the scene had projected themselves and this produced the true persons, the real situations, that Catherine had known. The projection had taken place completely or incompletely according to each case; the persons thus formed had shown themselves more or less substantially, more or less successfully done: this was the story of her life. But in the major circumstances she had always projected the scene in order that one might rediscover the origin of this or that one of her impulses. She had said of someone: "Now that I have met him, my life is going to change completely," or "From the day I first knew him my life was turned upside down." What an error! She should have said, "Because I had such and such needs, to play and to suffer, needs organized into several immutable figures, therefore I met him."

"The Lover-Death figure that signifies that I cannot love except with the accompaniment of death, and if possible by killing, was incarnated in Pierre Indemini. He was a handsome, weak creature promised to death, and I loved him for that very reason. I threw myself on love, I exhausted it, I behaved in such a way that love left me, I found love again, and I obtained death. But what am I doing today? I summon the Mongol or Luc Pascal; I am coarse and servile, I make him despise me, and I would like to profit from his cruelty to become a victim. After Indemini's death, when I had suffered enough, the lover I had lost assumed a divine character. It was the figure of the Lover-Christ. Without pity or charity, though he loves me, I want him to die; then I will turn him into a god. Did Pierre Indemini exist? I don't know, but my Indemini existed. When, after we started up again, 'he' demanded a new separation and the privation of all sexual relations—in the heart of love, who was casting the die? I alone. There I am again. '*Noli me tangere*—Do not touch me.' Soon after, he died. Who made him die? I made him die. In order to deify Pierre, I was capable of killing. There exists around us a great deal of the unknown, the mysterious. My strength is therefore certainly fatal. My love is therefore certainly murderous. For in the fatal figure I had at first formed, one will notice that there is Christ; and if I had entirely realized that part of my soul, I would have been a nun, a cloistered woman, I would have known how to pray; but no, I didn't realize it. So I had to stay with the theater of anger, of pain and fatality—with the bad figures. And as for him, he really—died.

"It's amazing that I can have all these thoughts without their being accompanied by remorse."

METRO DAYDREAM

This takes place in a car on the metro. The car is going fast and the walls of the car skim close to the cement walls of the tunnel. She is sitting at the front, close to the driver's booth. She is day-dreaming. She experiences a powerful and fierce feeling. She looks at the driver of the metro car. She feels something she has never felt before. She doesn't know how to think it and say it. The current is accelerating, that's all. The current is passing from her feet through her body and reaching her heart. The current—or maybe the concert, the music of the concert, for she can hear it perfectly, the music performed by a large orchestra accompanying vast choirs. Marvelously beautiful. What is the piece? The music moves away. With splendor, with regret. It seems to her that she is changing levels in her happiness without leaving her happiness, and here is the metro again. The metro procures for her the most intense pleasure of her life. Next to her a brown-haired man who is not looking at her; he is fat, a little coarse, something like an automaton. Catherine has lifted her right leg and she has laid the beautiful leg on the man's knees. The car is going fast. At the same time, on the other side is an elegant gentleman, tall and pale, whose features are uncertain. Catherine makes a move that is even bolder, she stretches out her beautiful torso, and lays her head between the elegant man's hands. Thus bestowed on the two men . . . The car races on.

Now Catherine's head is decorated, her hair is black and curled into numerous rosettes. In the middle of one rosette an eye opens, a third eye in addition to her eyes. The gentleman says to Catherine, so beautiful and happy, "See how pretty your eye is under the veil-ette"—he has an odd pronunciation—"under the viol-ette."

At these words, Catherine's happiness is complete, although she has understood that he meant to talk about violets; and remembering also another day, she thinks that Little X. has told her another story about violets. When the Father, said the Little One, bathed in the stream, he came out of the water offering his daughter a bouquet of violets.

"See how pretty your eye (your eye of love) is under the veil-ette." Violets, viol-ettes, you are hidden, inside the veil. But what exactly, sir, is this veil? It is your hair, the hair on your head. Ah, I understand, said Catherine, what that means, the violets, and I understand perfectly what the bouquet of violets was long ago! And since the elegant gentleman, like the man of long ago, was gathering the eye and the violets, she reached *as she understood* a paroxysm of happiness—but—it must be said—she owed the paroxysm to the other one, the brown-haired man, the one holding her leg.

Then, the picture having cracked, the various pieces disappeared. Sound came back. Everything was purer. Once again she began to hear the masses of the choir, and below it the themes of the orchestra. Catherine, tired from having been so powerful, fell asleep.

How One Wrestles
with the Angel

XVIII

MADEMOISELLE NOÉMI

My God, Mademoiselle Noémi had had a very good winter and had lacked for nothing in accordance with nature. Her breasts had swollen and turned pink, her figure had filled out, her flanks had developed, and her legs, which had been thin, were becoming pretty. She was conducting a transformation of her physical person, and she even seemed to be growing taller. She had given up the black that made her rather stand out; she was simply but elegantly dressed in dark clothes. Yet Mademoiselle Noémi was still prudent. Neither glory nor riches, such was still her maxim. But she had freedom, and she made use of it. She had settled nicely into her own home with the help and protection of M. Trimegiste. Since there was "nothing between them," no one could find fault. She was no longer a student, she had broken with that disreputable genre, and without listening to Catherine's suggestions had taken up typing. She was very proud of having become real in the Paris marketplace and thought that she could visit her friends Catherine and Flore as their equal.

Although she was undergoing corporeal changes, her rituals were the same: her coquetries with everyone, her childish mimicries, in particular, the movements of her mouth and the operation of her preferences in her friendships—it was always necessary that she prefer someone over all the rest and tell that person so. For the moment she preferred Catherine, after having preferred M. Trimegiste for a long time. And between M. Trimegiste and Catherine there had been a temporary Scottish student who said nasty things to her and whom she had very soon dismissed. (One would be wrong to think that Trimegiste's star had fallen. We have spoken of preferences, and M. Trimegiste, who is her fiancé represents something quite different. Oh, everything that gives us the certainty of being loved! It almost permits us to do without love and to enter into other feelings.)

For Mademoiselle Noémi (if we were to descend a little into the vast well of her days and nights) was, in short, "unhappy." Let us approach the "little point" where Noémi's destiny was still halted. The more time passed, the more Noémi suffered at this point; the less she moved, as she waited for the greatest event that ever was and that could contain a catastrophe. On this point— *virgo sum*—Noémi had too much to risk. And how alone she was! To whom could she confide such a feeling? Was she allowed to ask advice from Trimegiste, though she also cherished him like a father? No, she couldn't, could she? And on this point she was so occupied with waiting, having in her mind ideas which she ought to admit to at confession, that even her false mother, Catherine, couldn't help her. Besides, the people who approached Catherine at this time were unanimous in complaining about her and claimed that they had to endure inexplicable moods on her part. Noémi, though so sensitive, did not notice this uneasiness and felt nothing particular. Except . . . Noémi was very curious; she had highly developed senses, but the most developed was that of "seeing." That wasn't all, she also felt a *tenderness* endowed with an odd warmth: "I'm dying of tenderness for you!" From the depths of her deep prison, Noémi looked tenderly at Catherine, and in fact did not take her eyes off her. If Catherine reached her goal, this would also profit Noémi. Then there was the other side, the resentment. Noémi felt an instinctive resentment toward anyone who touched upon "the question," and this time it was Catherine in her entirety who was touching upon "the question." This was why Noémi tried to pinch Catherine's fingers in a drawer or make her slip in the middle of the stairway, but more often laid her head on Catherine's breast with an air of mute reproach.

So many changes of atmosphere must end in a tornado. Noémi sank into a depression. Then the "black teeth" came back, and the eyes almost crushed by tears. Noémi's falls were extremely rapid, vertical. Very soon she reached the point of saying with convincing force, "When do you want me to commit suicide?" The result of so many contrary efforts, in Noémi, was a desire to die, a thirst for nothingness. Ignorant of herself, her need to die came to surprise her "for the first time," with a frightful power, as we have said. While the demons were there, she "understood nothing about it" and yielded entirely to them. Catherine thought she was capable of someday carrying out the act. When Noémi talked about suicide, the most brilliant of fires filled her eyes. Sometimes the idea of suicide inspired a simulacrum and Noémi fell to the ground, as stiff as a board. It was impressive, and Catherine liked even better the scenes in which Noémi adopted plastic poses and contorted herself in a thousand ways.

One last thing put Mademoiselle Noémi in a dreadful position. She detested M. Pascal. For her, M. Pascal signified the intruder, the enemy. The truth is she had a horrifying weakness with respect to him. In the presence of M. Pascal, Noémi felt that what she desired most in the world, what she wanted immediately, and in the most pressing way, was for someone to make a child with her. Why fasten this beautiful dream on such a hateful man? Wouldn't Trimegiste, for instance, be very good for that, once he became her husband? No, no, it was *this man Pascal,* and it was Pascal and not the other who had the child-making power. Noémi imagined—height of horrors—M. Pascal's potency as a male, and she pictured to herself a measurement, a certain number of centimeters. Unfortunately, she did not know the number. She would have given everything to know it! At last, between her desire for the child and her curiosity about the number, Noémi thought she would go mad. It was certain that this child, coming from such a bandit, would not be made for her in the usual way. What a situation. Oh, what a horrible situation. What a peremptory reason this was for contemplating suicide! To love Catherine and to find herself so debased before Catherine's man. Anyway, it was impossible to conceive that an admirable woman like Catherine could give herself to that masculine brigand.

XIX

. . . Thus, in the middle of winter, it seemed to her that she was delivered.

After having recovered the story of the shepherd, rediscovered the Father; after having set down all her emotion, the worst and the best, the anguish and the hope, on the shoulders of a man, of a single man, of the only man who could save her and whom she adored for that reason, on Leuven's shoulders, in short—and after having seen the heavy, the intolerable thing move away and Leuven draw back also . . . Catherine was feeling better. Suddenly she was lighter. Her portrait, her confounded portrait, was clear, clear, complete. She said to herself that the larvae, the aborted creatures, the monsters with human faces, had disappeared, because they had been seen and judged by her: You don't scare me. She was at last going to know the truth and love life efficaciously. The traces of original sin were diminishing . . .

Yet what was Leuven asserting with his "Watch out, Madame!"? She obtained happiness in the image of the metro only through an artifice, he said, and if one looked at her playing the role of this metro, a role that signified for the first time the arrangements of her instinct after the profound upheaval, if one looked at her in this role, one saw a man rather than a woman, a low-level Don Juan. Catherine no doubt accepted what she had never accepted, but not altogether as a woman, with the artifice of a leg. "It's true, Sir," she answered, "that I have always had contempt for the condition of a woman." She unleashed a great tirade against women, those eternal objects. "For instance, in the case of Noémi, the thought that this girl is a cow is equivalent, for me, to the thought that she is charming." And it seemed to her that the famous image of the metro did not lack for cowlike charm itself! But M. Leuven stressed his distrust of a troublesome mechanism: Catherine did not accept herself as a woman.

A week later, the impression of security, contentment, and good solid ground under her feet seemed to lack force and to be unable to sustain itself. The subject felt failure gaining little by little, accompanied by the imagining of a "black hole." Sometimes her uneasiness stopped, the evil seemed overcome. Catherine, desperate, hung on. The clouds came back, piled up, rolled; and beneath them, the enormous Beast, with his hunger for suffering, which repeats the experience as many times as necessary. But when Leuven urged her to see clearly, she could distinguish only motions that turned, of which she saw only the speeds, flights into infinity of very small objects, then mixtures of sensations, a confusion among tastes, colors, and noises; lastly there occurred a sort of general announcement.

She was walking among these appearances—surprise, surprise. She was informed of their frightful but fictive nature and at the same time she experienced them as true. She was plunged in a fabric of feelings in which she did not yet exist, in the laboratory where what will be world and truth develops. More than fright, the state would cause her a great deal of sorrow: for in that case she was not delivered . . .

She remembered having been a believer. She saw herself once again at the church in Compesière before the choir, or in Abbé Cary's confessional, or at the Lord's Table. What a sweet spiritual smell and what internal truth reigned then! Was it necessary that so much grace should have been withdrawn? She could hear Abbé Cary, in his commentary on the sublime "penitent love" of Mary Magdalene, pronounce with extreme emotion the *Noli me tangere*. Catherine returned to a seventeenth-century sermon that she still loved: " . . . Still she saw Jesus Christ in the agonies of the Cross; still this last cry of her dying Spouse pierced not so much her ears as the depth of her soul . . . Still she heard the echoing of that killing word, intolerable to a loving heart: *Do not touch me.* Thus, her stricken love howled more than it sighed, and Jesus, pitiless, left her in her solitude . . . " Catherine's tears fell in memory on the dress she had worn as a child; and the profound exaltation, and the peace, intangible as well as insatiable, of the world according to the love of Jesus, showed themselves again to her heart. But alas, as a memory.

Impossible to reassemble the features of Abbé Cary, who had such importance for her. He was a village holy man. But he had accompanied her from afar, for a long time, and she recalled having dismissed him in the end with a telegram. She had certainly given him back his *noli me tangere!*

"The operation that is being performed on me now degrades me." An attempt to enter a church appeared grotesque to her; she went back out immediately. "I want to leave all that I have loved! Indemini, Flore, Pascal—I want to die for all those human beings. I want to be stripped of everything and go off alone. I see that I was deceived." What does that mean? One does not deceive oneself. What has been done is done and can no longer be undone. It is only necessary to realize it. "What became active was a part of oneself that can never be led astray: the part, indeed, that induces us to find or abandon God, to believe or cease to believe, to take this man or that woman, to set this goal before us." And would this part let protestations be heard? "What will you say, Magdalene, to Jesus, your dear lover? Will you complain that he deceived you? No, no: he does not deceive us; or, if he deceives us, it is in another way."

O nostalgia.

M. Leuven showed by his obstinate attitude, by his obstinate attitude, said Catherine, that he saw no other way for her than that of *opening her heart*. M. Leuven denied religion.

Her acts with Pascal disgusted her.

Damned Pascal! As though her feelings for Pascal were already covered over by an immense layer of oblivion, she was obliged to summon memories of him as distant as those of her life as a little girl. Yet she continued to perform the acts! How frightfully ugly was her soul? She perceived very clearly that when she had begun making love with him during the preceding autumn, she had not concerned herself with the soul, nor with establishing anything in the soul between her and him. "So I took him as an erotic implement and not as a human soul."

"Friend or enemy? Speak. Who are you? I badly need a friend." No, she did not need a friend. She finally had to know what this barbarian was, this outlaw, this poet, tool of the devil, for whom beauty had a face of death! Surely, in the mind of someone like Pascal the universe was an inclined plane that descended toward the great tomb, and before dying on this plane one seized things by war. But sad eternity in the end would win out over the warriors, as it mocked, debased their war itself! "He horrifies me," thought Catherine. "How is it possible that he was able to please me and satisfy me?"

She saw the cadaverous head of a woman, mouth open, as though cut out of paper, her eyes rolling toward the corners of her eyelids: her, pressed against Pascal.

She had met him on the sidewalk and they were going home together. "I walk close to him submissively, like his wife. I could just as well brandish his severed head in my fist and I would be happier about it." His wife—so degrading was the feeling that it would have been better to say his daughter. A moment later, Luc Pascal, point-blank, asked her for money. She handed the sum over to him as soon as they were home. Catherine liked money when it passed from one hand to another. And in Catherine's smile, Luc encountered the idea of giving her the order (she had scarcely undressed), the order he knew she would obey: Get down on your knees! She went down on her knees without even answering, with delight. She stayed there all exposed, surrounded by air. She took pains to lift the mass of her breasts with her shoulder muscles, so that the man's gaze would not suffer. Oh, Oh!

The Mongol walked back and forth, his eyes full of firmness and satisfaction. At last the Mongol *spat on the floor.* Then he dismissed her. He said to her: "That's enough. Go away."

After recovering her freedom, she felt tired, as though at the onset of a serious illness. She took a few steps in the stairway and stopped right away to think. The words *"That's it exactly!"* resonated in her heart with a noise full of echoes. "She really wanted people to treat her so badly. She liked insults. How she obeyed. How hard and strong he was. How happy she was. He could do anything to her. How ignoble it was!" etc.

Because she had been happy on her knees, she no longer had the means to reject him; but she had to know clearly that the demon of destruction lived in that man. *Danger. Danger of death!* Oh why did he want so much to kill? Would he have behaved in the same way and would he have developed the same joy in destroying if he had not sensed in her the appeal for destruction and the joy in being destroyed and, on the other hand, the mysterious effort, still too weak, that was being made in favor of her life against these same demons which had been in control for so long? Do you want to live, do you want to die?—such was the question he brought to her. "Oh, oh . . . if you go that far, I certainly long for death."

She certainly longed for death!

The Little One displayed an extreme worry about the power of the Mongol. "Danger, danger!" she cried. "Are you going to be the victim of that pervert, of that wicked man who wants to prevent your salvation, of that sick man who slips his malady into yours and pulls you down? If you have done something stupid with him, you want to let the thing remain unimportant. Hey, do you know who he is? The angel of death. I know him perfectly. Where he lives is full of coffins. You're not going to hand over your life to the angel of death disguised? Are you? Come on, tell me."

"Just the opposite—you must use this new *trial* to open your heart a little more and make progress in your purifications. You must use everything."

XX

THE COOK

A fat woman in bed. At the foot of the bed, as always, unknown people were standing guard. Catherine's hair hung loosely down her back and pulled together toward her forehead, as was the style at her age: twelve or thirteen. In her hand the little girl was holding a large, open book: she was learning something.

The fat woman resembled M. Leuven at the time when he was a woman. She had large dark eyes and her hair, especially, was dark. Catherine looked at the fat woman and went up to her, in a natural way. Because she was embracing her *out of duty*, suddenly, whoops, Catherine slipped and fell on her; and so clumsily that she certainly must have hurt her. The fat woman, without moving, began to speak: "No, you didn't injure me, my child; I have no feeling in my left side. I think you must know that?" Catherine said yes; swinging her head, pain constricted her heart, and everything disappeared in an instant.

Under the influence of the shock, as after the arrival of a woman intruding, she thought of the *the fat women in her life*. The most recent and the closest was indeed Leuven. And the first—"whom one mustn't talk about"—was, she had always been told, small and thin. (She would never know anything about that since she had no photograph and not the slightest recollection. In Catherine's memory most women seemed fat; they were cooks. She would not have been able to say how the thing came to be true, even when the woman was small and thin.) If she was so afraid of touching that fat Leuven-woman, did this mean Catherine desired his death? But one couldn't even kill her, the fat woman felt nothing. She was therefore an untouchable! She was impure, and one could do nothing against her. She was holy, being so fat. She was amazing. She was. . . .

Other fat women appeared and said again to Catherine: I am recalling myself to you. These fat women—now, who was it? Surely not her mother. "My mother was small and thin." "Couldn't I be one of your relatives?" Ah—one of my mother's sisters. But was she as fat as that? No, but she was fat and had dark hair, and she was a fat, dark-haired woman, and she was a fat, pregnant, dark-haired woman.

Taboo.

Who had spoken that word without Catherine's knowledge, a word she had read many times and whose complicated meaning she did not understand?

She had to get away from the horrible subject of this fat woman, but just one last idea: if one reflected carefully on the phenomenon of her side that felt nothing, one thought, she has a side that feels nothing so that one can't hurt her. But what if it so happened that Catherine herself was the fat woman? Then the unfeeling side meant something quite different: "That doesn't hurt me" or "That must not be allowed to hurt me," and finally, by degrees, "I have adjusted myself so that that will not hurt me at all." This was what the little girl was learning in the book. And the fat woman did not become human, because now she had become Catherine and her mother, one on top of the other. One therefore saw a pregnant Catherine to whom the child would do no harm, since no child would ever come out of Catherine.

"Of course," cried Little X., "didn't the child die in the left side? Then he won't do any harm."

Taboo! Taboo!

* * *

These preliminaries heralded the arrival of the Mother, who moved toward Catherine slowly and cautiously, dark, not so much from her mourning as from a sort of invisibility of her face and her body.

But first, the persons standing guard next to the bed no longer left Catherine alone for even a moment. By day, by night, they were there. Their presence was much more authoritarian than that of the gentle Little X., to whom they had certainly given the order to go away. The bodyguards arrived when they wanted to and "went inside"; one could not get rid of them.

They went so far as to touch and jostle Catherine when the work was not going the way they wanted it to, when "the task was too difficult," and Catherine was not obeying or understanding quickly enough. The task is the necessity presented by the operation, in which one is locked; which means that in the same minute when one is thinking, "This time it's finished, finished, I won't go any farther!" one also thinks, "But I have to go even farther." And so the dark men, with round arms and legs, flank you closely; they climb the steps of the staircase, on the step above and on the step below, at the same time as you. At M. Leuven's, happily, they remain seated in the waiting room. So one can quarrel bitterly over the price, over the value (?) of the thing, over the possibility of finishing. One can shout, one can shed tears. One can haggle interminably (in order not to see the somber dark woman who is coming near).

Yet M. Leuven answers forcefully! "You are in *your situation.* I'm not one of the people accompanying you. You would no longer be able to extricate yourself, having the gang of them against you, without my help." "If you detest me, it's because you feel steeped in your guilt vis-à-vis the gang." "If you are afraid, it's because you have a fund of hatred that comes to you from the gang and that you project against me." "If you have submitted without agreeing, it's because you are playing the game of this gang, which in actuality doesn't exist." Oh, how necessary it is to be encouraged this way and beaten this way, in order to produce something!

THE STATION

"Are you still acting?" the producer said to her.

"No, sir, I'm not doing any more of that, not at all."

"Well, for your pleasure just look at this pretty film for me."

A station. The iron architecture is monumental, but hidden toward the top by a thick substance. The space is limited. The platforms entirely dark, of the same darkness as the air. They are empty, deserted. Forgotten suitcases here and there. The dust is falling onto the ground.

A stranger is walking quickly, carrying piles of packages in her two hands and dressed in a checked "mackintosh" of an unlikely but very comfortable cut. It's her. It's really her. Even though she has never seen such a large station, she knows that she is in Vienna's West Bahnhof.

There is no train by the platform.

The mysterious woman who is not taking any train goes into the waiting room. The waiting room has a clock that shows three o'clock in the morning. The face is enormous, and while she reads the hour she sees beds, four beds, arranged against the wall.

This is a dormitory where people are lying down. The traveler occupies one of the beds and lies down; and she even finds that she has been lying there for some time.

She is ill. She knows, in an absolutely sure, interior fashion, that this time she is going to die. She is in the bed for that. The power of the ineluctable gives our acts great simplicity. She is going to die, she knows it, so everything is simple. She doesn't want to discuss anything anymore. She doesn't remain lying down, it isn't worth it, she is sitting. She sees very clearly into the phenomena of death that are imminent. There is nothing easier than to die. What am I saying—she is sitting? Gradually the traveler has seen herself in her bed, dying, has looked at herself in her bed, has seen that she was there, and has moved away from the bed and from herself, without ceasing to look at the bed and know that she was in it. Thus distanced from herself, she sees that the bed is filled with the dying woman, dirty and disgusting; then, surreptitiously, so intense is her repugnance, she slips into the next bed.

From the next bed, once again, she sees what was once herself and what will soon die, what she has left. She knows that over there she is forty-five years old and that she is her cousin Flore Migett's cook. She is a fat, dark-haired woman. And since she is the cook, fat and dark, little by little she feels something else. The cook she is is not positively the cook, and it is not her mother either, no, it is *her antecedent on earth*. She comes from there. It isn't she, that old horror! It isn't she, but she comes from it.

She moves still farther away from the horrible dying woman. She walks in the opposite direction, toward the other wall, where the fireplace is. Close to the fireplace, someone, in a deep silence. Catherine, out of the bed, takes two steps and considers. With his back to the fireplace, resting his elbows on the marble, stands a Male Presence. He is wearing an elegant, foppish suit; in his right hand he is holding gloves, in his left, a rattan cane; his handsome pale face, framed by his black hair and his little New-gate frill, is surmounted by a vast top hat with curved edges, in the style of 1840. Nonchalant, the personage manifests a free power, superior in essence. Everything he looks at he sees from above; and in a transcendent light that belongs to him in his own right, he observes what cannot fail to happen.

In fact it will happen.

The old woman opens her mouth; she has a single big, tusk-like tooth in front. Some blood comes out; blood in clots, a quantity of coagulated blood falls from that mouth. The wretched woman is in the throes of death, it's the end. The tooth is still visible. Catherine is glued to the wall with terror. The man by the fireplace attentively follows what is happening. He looks fixedly at Catherine, and after Catherine, he looks fixedly at the dying woman. The Male Presence in the large hat says simply to Catherine, "Kill her."

The order is very clear. "Kill her."

She must obey. She must go ahead and do it. The order is majestic, and what is more, so comprehensible. "Kill her!" One approaches, wondering if the earth will be firm enough. It hurts horribly. But this is the order that one can't avoid: Kill her.

And she *doesn't dare!* Why is it that she *cannot manage* to kill that wretched old woman—who is dying anyway? The Male Presence observes her with increased attention, if that is still possible. Catherine is upon the old woman. She is there. She applies her hands to the neck, and she probably squeezes the neck with iron fingers, the best she can, to achieve the result, but the atmosphere becomes confused because Catherine feels sick, and one can no longer distinguish in the confusion of blood and hands what is true from what is not. And perhaps, in the end, she has indeed . . .

. . . At first it's a green light, a phosphorus green, that spreads gently. It's as fresh as spring grass. Then it seems to be a beast.

The beast can fly the way insects do, but it is large like a giant mammal. Its species is unknown. It is the *new being*. But it is Catherine, in her inner being, who arranges her thoughts and her ornaments and, metamorphosed, at last shines with an unequaled brilliance. She is the one who moves her paws delicately in the paradisiacal light and bobs her head, that of a gracious ichthyosaur, and remains thus, survivor of the world which, with its nightmarish shadows, has entirely disappeared.

XXI

FONS VITAE

Her emotion had not yet subsided when the image was already disappearing. "I'm going to have to write," she thought, "because memory isn't enough anymore."

Only the Little One claimed to see something. M. Leuven, a very short time after, was inclined in the same direction as the Little One. According to them, one could recognize a very serious phenomenon, which in its seriousness truly deserved to be called "the most important one."

"You're certainly doing me a lot of good!" Catherine grumbled. "Tell me the hidden meaning instead, the exact meaning, and why it hurts so much."

"The meaning is: live, on pain of death."

"Pretty truth! And for a year now this is all anyone has talked to me about."

"One has to live or one has to die. One day truly the thing *happened*."

"You're very profound! You aren't teaching me anything."

"Birth."

"Okay, what about birth?"

"Birth in which life does not want to be life."

"A very sad birth."

"Yours. And today imitates yesterday."

"Look, let's imagine my birth. I knew nothing about life, nothing about death; and I supposedly wanted death? That's stupid."

"*Culpa.*"

"Oh . . . you frighten me." Then: "Let's go on," said Catherine. "I'm quite willing that death should stop me one day and plunge me into the unknown. I'm quite willing to admit that I'm afraid of death and that I am constructing all sorts of follies around this subject. But that death should be in me, should be me?"

"*Think* as you like about death, but there is life and death."

Catherine, brought back to the shock she had felt when the Little One had said "*Culpa,*" experienced slowly, heavily, and nebulously an idea, more or less this: that life corrupted by death would be the nature of original sin. *She had not had life, she had only had death.*

"So will you tell me how this horrible birth . . . "

"Quite possibly. We have to dig down further."

"I am a living woman!"

"On top, yes, on the surface . . . "

"Explain the dream now!"

"The fat woman is woman: your mother and you. Everything is holy and impure because of what she does. She is bleeding. As for you, you come out of the mother's belly, you don't want to live, and you try to kill all that in order to live!"

The powers of nature at war on all sides, there was no more Catherine. One would scarcely have recognized the physical form of this woman. One would have looked upon this whimpering creature with pity, probably with disgust. But in any case one would have felt, just looking at her, a horrifying fear. Ugly, this sniveling woman, but no longer the way one single man cries: the way all men cry. Abominable, swollen, she twisted her limbs in silence: the man who is obliged to live, having been unaware that he was being born, to whom birth was funereal, and who without having lived is soon going to be annihilated—with whom will he lodge the claim for his despair?

"Memories of limbo . . . gray . . . red . . . Fountain of life, heat . . . Heat, opacity, tenderness . . . Opacity, trust, rupture, revolt, cold, horror . . . Contact, anguish . . . Negation . . . Separation after abomination."

* * *

"It's true, materially I am alive; I'm not committing suicide." But she was living in the negation of life; thus she was living with death inside her.

And here she is when she comes back to life a little. She says insulting things to Flore. She refuses to receive the Mongol, slams the door on him; she fails to keep her appointments with Leuven and does not telephone; she spits on Noémi and company from afar. As for the old principles, the myths, love, Indemini . . . She is overcome with rage, she hurls herself at these idols, she tears them limb from limb. A wild animal is no more ferocious than this woman. You say a wild animal? But she is weeping, she does nothing but weep. She has decomposed into tears. It's a coffin of water. All of this takes place implacably in her and despite her. Life and death are awaiting a victim. Who will win out?

She is haunted by the coffin. The syllable "cof" in coffin grasps her under the chest and stifles her. She feels her own decomposition; the nauseating smell, familiar and general, the smell *of* the cadaver, which has become her smell, suffocates her. The smell takes her place, the smell fights with her for all eternity. And here she is, outside in an immense Paris cemetery; she sees a tombstone under the rain. The letters "Catherine Crachat" are already fading. The dampness around the dead people is horrifying. The water passes, eventually, through the wood, through the lead. It's a battle between the water and the gas, between the dampness and the smell. She is in a coffin of water for all eternity. A coffin of water . . . but has she ever left it? She is—where she was. Nothing has happened—no life . . .

No one . . .

No one from the earth or the heavens . . . No knight-errant . . . No Jesus Christ . . . In our time people don't get brought back to life anymore.

The images went away. The anguish, as it shrank, appeared distant. Catherine's back and legs hurt; she stayed in bed. The light of a gloomy winter day pained her nerves terribly, and she couldn't tolerate an electric lightbulb any better; complicated shivers, whose mechanical displacement she watched, started from the back of her neck and went all the way down to her feet: some were large waves, and those could stop on the way; others, delicate, delicate and rapid, ran all the way to the end. She was so *broken* that, although she did not demand the slightest effort from her arms and legs, her forehead was covered with sweat, as though the limit of her strength had been exceeded long before.

After a week in this state, suddenly she felt her body become afraid. It was a precise fear, a fear of the body. The fear became panic. There was a rout of the forces of the body. The frontier was no longer maintained, nor the land guarded. It was after that that she noticed blood flowing. She was losing copious amounts of blood. An attack of vertigo made the whole room move forward toward the left, caught it, sent it off again to the left. Bells were ringing. While she applied her last energy to grasping the necessary objects and calling for help, and while Flore appeared, and soon after the doctor, she was entirely inside the feeling of fear, and she did not even suffer anymore, the fear anesthetized her; this to such a degree that the hemorrhage could not legitimize a fear like that, as they pointed out to her. In her entire life, Catherine had never known so shameful a trouble. Then she saw once again the scene in which the fat woman vomited blood, and she was completely certain that that dream was premonitory and that it was informing her of what was going to be her fate. In the dream, the fat woman dies. The hemorrhage continued, the fear did not yield. At last she understood that she was representing through her body what she was thinking, deep inside herself, about childbirth. This horror, this gluey blood, were the real replicas of the dream, which then cracked in its mass of images and gave up its meaning, yielded it, vomited it also, the way the dragon of the legendary forest is obliged to give up the ring: and it was the old horror of being born of a woman in blood, indicated by the open mouth, and the tooth with its sexual appearance.

XXII

NOTHING LEFT

—I have nothing left. Why live?

—Why are you here?

—I am here as a consequence of what has happened. But everything is finished. I don't love anything anymore. I have nothing left.

—Why are you so greedy?

—Greedy! But I only have what everyone has!

—You have exactly what everyone has.

—What everyone has . . . what is that for me now?

—You have turned the question around.

—I'm going to leave!

—All right, leave, if that's what you really want. *Where* do you want to go?

—I don't know. Everything is a lie.

—So you see you have to stay.

—Where?

—Here.

—Your system is vile. You ought to be taken to court.

— . . .

—You ought to be attacked before the law. You lock people up. You extort their wills.

—You mean you're reproaching me for not having forced your will out of you.

—You have taken from me: everything. What have you given me in exchange? Health, maybe? Excuse me while I laugh. I almost died a week ago. Happiness, maybe? I'm a fountain of tears. You have exposed me entirely naked and you have displayed my shame. And then? Won't you put a bandage on that wound? But there isn't anything further that you can do; you haven't the means.

—I can see that your health has improved. You're entrenching yourself in the fortress of your former person.

—You're watching me die! I'm dying anyway. Not as quickly as my work in film showed me to be dying, not as quickly, unfortunately, as I would deeply like to, but I am dying.

—You've holed yourself up in that stronghold of yours. Come on out of there.

—That means that when one wants to study the habits of a snail, one doesn't pull on its antennae, one waters the ground all around it. I tried to get myself sideswiped by a car again. It didn't work. Too bad. But it almost worked.

—You failed in your attempt.

—And despite everything I failed in my attempt. You're gloating.

—Then you have only to stay here and continue.

—I tell you I haven't got anything left. I'm completely naked, flat on the ground, like a stiff. Even my motion has been taken away from me, even my breathing, even my heart has been taken away! It's the pulmonary artery thing! All that about the pulmonary artery! Oh, oh! A nice mess! A nice mess! Let me cry.

"I've had it. Anyone can take over my life for the asking. But it isn't worth what it costs in feed. I had a love, a religious love. Ha, ha! They showed me that it was only a dead man. Oh what a joke, I told myself. I had a friend, a comfortable friend for always. Now we are like two cats and we spit furiously at each other. If I was so mistaken, I thought, why not try another man? But scarcely was he in my bed before I saw in his eyes the green glow of crime; oh that man, and you took care to tell me that I was the one who handed him his horrible revery. After that, there's no point in trying any further. I had a job, and some renown; if the quality was not equal to the quantity, still I was famous, they liked me. I have lost everything. I have no more money. The last I have is for you. I kept in my memory the touching image of a father whom life took away from me. You showed me a gloomy comedy, and that in his place I had put a grotesque statuette for whom I had dirty feelings. My mother I didn't know; you made me see her in her true form: a dead woman. The mother is mortal and she kills, and the maternal belly is a diet of filth. So what are you going to do with me after having dishonored me in my most sacred affections? Come on, explain yourself, once and for all. Is there a tragedy I'm not aware of? Did my mother kill me at birth? As I was being born did I kill my mother? Or since I am *no longer* that old woman, must I die in order to be something else, for example, to have a child? You know very well it's too late.

"Well? Well? What are you doing? Time is passing. My desolation grows deeper, like an abyss. You will never pull me out of it. You ought to be prosecuted in court."

(Who had fallen into whose trap?)

* * *

Soon she found herself face to face with two very small personages, placed in the landscape like two hard stones. He, dressed in a putty-colored suit of a very proper cut, remained completely motionless. She, on the other hand, wore a loose skirt and a gray Inverness cape; she was not, as he was, like a shop-window mannequin. The two of them thus face to face, nothing let one know what they wanted. The wind lifted the cape. It lifted it higher than their heads, so that the cape resembled a snail shell that descended very slowly when the wind left it a little. At this moment a voice said, "When the collar of the cape has fallen back completely, then *the word* will be found." But how the wind kept on blowing! The wind would begin blowing again all the more vigorously as soon as the enormous cloak was about to stay still a little.

The two personages changed into three or four women of proportions greater than normal. They had the perfect majestic beauty inherent in painted figures. Never had one seen women more superb, more sensual, with muscular movements more expressive, in their haunches, backs, chests, and legs. Never had one seen women who were more women, who expressed prouder obedience to the laws of femininity. The air was redolent of them, full of the fragrance of their nature. Never had there been a more convincing marvel. Their relationship contained an admirable principle. For the invariably rapid light bathed them in an atmosphere of ethereal time, but while they moved also for one another, and the trees bent immense boughs in their direction, the duration of the trees and of the space did not have the same value as the duration of the goddesses; everything changed visibly without ceasing to be invariable. Each goddess, in her honeylike hands, was holding a decorated box, and each of the boxes was decorated in a particular fashion. Each moving her arms in her particular space held her box out in an empty motion to her neighbor, and received from the latter her other box in exchange. The boxes, though immobile, circulated from hand to hand, and the boxes that traveled for the eye of the observer expressed, relative to the base of the light, certain things, for the goddesses through these exchanges made their thoughts known to each other. *The word* of the universe, in various forms, was contained in the boxes. A word for gathering, dissolving, creating, believing, and loving was inside the boxes. It was the word of a magnetic structure and it was the word of a kiss; it was the vocable of life. Anyway, it did not seem that the most important thing was to seize the word on the wing: to our understanding, it was probably unknowable. What was much more essential, rather, was the incessant motion of the women with the trees and boxes, the hints they made, their mysterious arrangements for continually passing each other the boxes that contained the precious Word, and, at the same time, all this in a general repose and complete immobility.

XXIII

A PERSON IN GOOD HEALTH

"You must go and see Noémi."

It was like an order that had appeared to issue, this morning, from the basin in her bathroom while she was washing; she couldn't dream of shirking it, however unhappy she was at that moment. She had to go to Noémi's place because certain things were happening there, yet she had no idea what was required of her. The order she had received that morning, unexpectedly appearing in the basin, meant that our responsibilities do not release us so easily and that one can certainly plunge into oneself all the way down to the abyss and almost die, while on the other hand that abyss can't be taken into consideration when something important is involved, like going to see Noémi.

Luc Pascal had informed against Noémi. He described how, as he happened to go to Noémi's to propose some work to her, he

had knocked at the door two or three times instead of ringing—
"a bad habit he had picked up in his house, where all the door-
bells were out of order." And what had he found? Mademoiselle
Noémi in the most suggestive of costumes.

"Well, what costume?" Catherine had said.

"Go there and see with your own eyes, it would be better. I
leave you the pleasure of the surprise. And I don't need to tell you
who these preparations were for. *She was expecting him.*"

Catherine went to Noémi's, and it was early in the afternoon.
"At this hour," she was thinking, "I won't find anything. I won't
find anything, I hope." She knocked at the door twice without
using the doorbell, "as it was agreed with that wicked Mongol."
Her heart was beating hard, because "in our life strange things
are always happening on stairways." The door opened halfway.
Just enough to show that a thick curtain was hung behind it.
Noémi Parchemin's inane, sugary voice, addressing the person
outside, could be heard. "Is it you, dear friend?" she said.

Catherine answered harshly, "It's me, Catherine."

"Oh no!" cried Noémi. The door closed and the safety bolt
turned inside.

Then Noémi's voice could be heard again, through the door,
"Actually, it doesn't matter to me," and the bolt turned back the
other way. Catherine entered, still hesitating. In the typist's room,
copies lay in folders on the furniture; Noémi was not visible.
Noémi appeared in an embrasure. Noémi was more than nude,
for the mixture of nudity and clothing was much more striking
than a body in the state of nature. It was certainly a nude rear
end that she placed on her chair, and bare thighs that she crossed,
as she looked at Catherine with a strange assurance: that which
comes from the certainty of being *understood.*

Catherine observed that this time the dream was remarkably
solid. "I'm dreaming, I'm dreaming, I'm having a nightmare,"
she said to herself to calm herself. Noémi, completely motionless,

was breathing. Nothing underneath her blouse! Nothing but skin from her hips all the way down to that indecent sock; panties like a zephyr, better to have none on at all. And roses in her hand! She had roses in her hand. But reality fell back into place when Noémi announced cynically, "I thought it was Trimegiste, but he is quite late." Could Noémi be mad?

"You little tart . . . You little tart!" Catherine, to her surprise, did not succeed in interjecting these words with any severity. She could not make her feel that she found her disgraceful. Catherine was sweating with shame. Catherine wondered only: When will I be able to get out and stop looking at a sight so filled with accusation against me? This caused Noémi to pass quickly from an initial situation characterized by mild displeasure to one of out-and-out pleasure, since she was showing herself to Catherine for the first time and by this means she "had" Catherine, as they put it. Thus she said, with shining eyes: "If he comes, we won't open the door. It will be just for the two of us, today." Ceasing to imitate wax, Noémi moved, and decided to make some tea.

Catherine was sitting down.

She was reciting the confiteor. "I am to blame, great is my blame." Yet now Catherine cast at her in a snarling voice, "You're sleeping with him?"

"Dear God, how dreadful!" said Noémi. "Sleeping with a man—who do you take me for?"

"But—that outfit."

"We love each other," she confessed sincerely. "I truly hope he will marry me."

Our heart filled with discouragement. "To say," thought Catherine, "that I will continue to drag along this person Noémi."

"You called me *tart* just now," Noémi resumed, while pouring the tea. "What you meant was nasty slut, right?"

"Yes, yes," said Catherine.

"Well you shouldn't! I'm not that, any more than any other

woman, for instance, a woman who doesn't do what I'm doing but carries all that inside herself!"

Noémi sat her unclothed rear end on Catherine's knees and, taking hold of Catherine's shoulders with her little iron hands, kissed her over and over again.

THE RIBBONS

Her case seemed desperate to her.

What had been attempted in favor of her life was turning violently against her life. Let us recapitulate.

They had tried to draw her profound appetite toward the man and toward the child who is the natural consequence, given that for a woman all joys, all strengths, had to have passed once through that necessary channel; they had tried to cure her of her sterility, but they had not obtained her firm belief, and moreover her age no longer allowed her the experience of it. They had gravely troubled her by showing her obscene photographs. They had taken from her almost everything by presenting to her what she had done in her life, either as a dismal automatism or as a puppet-show parody. They were going to leave her face to face with a horrifying *nothingness*. They had not stopped their demolition inside her, and what workers were ever going to come and rebuild? If one shadow still rose up to fight against the Nothingness, that shadow was Fault: unanimous, universal, one could almost love it; but when all was said and done, she was in agreement with Nothingness.

. . . .

And in that memorable session in which she saw M. Leuven for the last time, she spoke straight out to him and described the despair that filled her, and she concluded, "I don't care!" She still had a little laughter in the corner of her lips to proclaim: I don't care. "I have nothing left, I'm nothing anymore—I don't care." Her eyes, her poor eyes, were aimed in the direction of that man, but not at all like loaded pistols. She repeated two or three times, not in order to sentimentalize but to be done with it: "I don't care."

M. Leuven seemed like one of those captains armored in a slicker confronting the high seas during a storm. He also resembled a fat woman, the fat mother.

She said, in a voice that was low, sickly, but absolutely sincere: "I would like you to kill me. Kill me."

He answered like clockwork, "You mean you would like to kill me."

Catherine's heart leaped crazily in her chest, and she almost lost consciousness in a sort of fit of dizziness. "You don't understand me! You won't ever understand me!

"If I asked you to kill me, that can't mean the opposite: that I want to kill you."

"If you ask *me* to kill *you,* that means that, not being able to free yourself from the effect a certain person has on you . . . " M. Leuven adopted a scolding voice to say, "You understand clearly whom I am talking to at this moment?" and went on: " . . . Not being able to free yourself from the effect a certain person has on you, you think of murder; but not wanting to kill, you are led to desire that the weapon be turned against you."

"I don't believe you! When one desires death, one doesn't want to kill."

M. Leuven repeated in his scolding voice, "You understand clearly whom I am talking to at this moment?"

Catherine was silent, oppressed.

"Why does one desire death?" asked M. Leuven. "Because one is crushed and mortified, and the pleasure is no longer great enough. If one had other means of regaining the advantage, one would not ask for death. One of the means, the simplest, consists in getting rid of the person or persons who are bothering one, who are hurting one. But if one can't even free oneself of the hated personage enough to strike the blow at him, then one holds onto the idea of death, one puts it in his hands, and one says to him: you, strike me. That way the desire for death returns to its point of departure."

"Your explanation is absurd. I need to disappear; I don't have the strength to carry out my desire. I dream that you have become enough of a friend to me to agree to help me do it."

"You have first of all a *need to kill.*"

"What grievance would I have against you to the point of wanting to kill you?"

"I represent all your hatred, your misery, your disappointment. I represent that blur of life and death from which you do not want to separate yourself but which can't continue any longer."

In fact, M. Leuven was not thinking of telephoning the police. He was calm, once again, like the deep-sea captain.

"Yes," Catherine confessed, "death is certainly a sin and an evil."

She felt a relaxation taking place, similar to the opening up of a frightful spring. It was true that she had wanted to kill him. She still wanted to. The relaxation of the frightful spring occurred more and more, without her being able to discover what was relaxing, nor predict where this relaxation would take her. She experienced first a profound amelioration. The relaxation was long, long in being fully realized. At last it was done. She was relaxed.

Why this majestic relaxation?

Catherine ceased to be afraid once she resigned herself to wanting to kill Leuven; wanting to kill this individual for what he was himself and for the immense quantity of things he represented. In fact, she was killing him. The murder took place somewhere, and a mysterious sweetness . . .

PASSAGE JOUFFROY

It must be said that when she came out of Noémi's house she had walked aimlessly. When night fell, she found herself in the busy streets of the center. She heard a discordant, continuous noise that she falsely attributed to her ears; she saw lines of blocked cars start off. It was hard for her to move along the sidewalks because everything was completely obstructed. Certain more inso-lent wheels even tried to tear her from her refuge. Bars of multi-colored, dancing light streaked the sky, or rather the walls of the buildings at each story, in order to force her to read all kinds of slogans. There were gaping cafés where strange sorts of people seemed to live in an atmosphere of fury, and one could not understand either their attitude or their occupation. Between the sticky wooden pavement and the pieces of commercial informa-tion, between the street and the barroom, between the people and the cars, there was similitude and common substance; one left one and easily entered the other, for the whole thing was like the matter circulating in a very large intestine. Catherine did not move under her own impetus, she was pushed. Here everything was done together and in the common substance: for instance, looking into the furiously lit windows of underwear, bronzes, or umbrellas; going, coming back, crossing; stopping like everyone else in front of the billboards of the movie theaters.

She reached the large boulevards. The figures followed one another so closely that to look at them as they filed by induced a sort of giddiness. She found herself at the entrance to a glittering archway. I don't know how many small lights formed round and concentric necklaces against a background of glass and mirrors;

the crowd circulated, and in front of the shops the space filled and emptied. She went in under the lights. What she had seen at Noémi's place remaining in her head, in the midst of the crowd, like a very real thing, it seemed to her that everything she perceived of this arcade, so dazzling and so old-fashioned, was unreal; and yet, one thing and another came together, she felt a single emotion. Her emotion grew after the fourth shop, because she saw directly in front of her a cooked mutton chop on a plate on a bistro table. She remembered having seen it before entering the arcade. An eye swam in the air above the chop, and it soon passed over the chop, the plate, and the table.

Catherine was horrified by what she saw, and she walked down the arcade. The mutton chop made her think of Adam's rib, and surely this involved the question of women again, and a woman, in truth, was no more than a filthy cutlet: a wretched bit of food served in a bistro; for immediately and distinctly she saw before her her aunt, whom she had quite forgotten! This sister of her mother's, whom she had so completely forgotten, yes, Catherine had been taken to visit her during the first years after they arrived in Paris; a rather overweight woman with brown hair, vulgar; and—as it happens!—Catherine was forever bundled into the Passage Jouffroy with this aunt, since the latter lived at number 9, and—my God!—she and her aunt had gone into the shops together, to this postage-stamp vendor, to this printer of visiting cards, into a hairdresser's who used to be where the bookseller now was, and—all of a sudden Catherine stopped.

She was in front of a rather dark shop without a door in which peculiar beings were bustling around. They wore green aprons and their faces were lusterless, gray. Three steps led up to a platform with five armchairs in a line, as though for five condemned people (they had been of red-painted wood, but filth had rendered them as black as pitch). Two of the chairs were empty; the other three had men in them. Around the latter revolved the sickly personages in green aprons, spitting into their fingers! It was the shoeshine place. So this was where the horrible shoeshine man had been, who used to frighten her so, her hand in her aunt's! But her aunt's husband was a businessman of some kind, with an office in the rue Bergère, and it hadn't gone well, he had been put in prison at Mazas. He was in prison at Mazas, and her aunt always told about how she would go to see him, and how the corridors were long; the corridors of the Mazas prison were interminable, filthy, disgusting. This fat woman adored him, of course, and while he was in prison she "spent her nights" stringing little black pearls, by the meter, for hat manufacturers, for in those days women wore hats made of jet and pearls. It was just in front of the shoeshine store, in the Jouffroy arcade, that her aunt told her the story of the *prison*—here, in this very spot—but at the time her aunt was telling her this, Catherine could not squeeze her aunt's hand to comfort her, because the unfortunate woman, who still loved her husband despite the prison, had been afflicted with a repulsive case of eczema on her hands!

. . . While she remained petrified in front of the boot polisher's, Catherine heard a proposition in her ear; this woke her up, and she fled. Running under the lights of the arcade, she crossed the street and ended up in a second arcade much worse than the first. Here everything was truly a dark prison. The walls were lined with human wretchedness. It was gloomy. Suits of armor, strongboxes stared at the intruder, but also books with scatalogical titles decorated with little women, titles that spoke to her confidentially; and more strongboxes, nothing but strongboxes! Catherine sensed her exhaustion. But she had to walk, walk, even if the sweat was coming out of her hair and running down her temples. She had to walk, she had to run: nothing could have stopped her. And here was a mannequin store! Displayed here was a row of women of different sizes, made of a shiny substance rather like biscuit, most of them with little girls' bodies wearing only stockings and a hat, and they were all smiling in a perverse way. Catherine felt an intense heat on her hands; her hands, which she examined in the light, were covered with an eruption of red spots. Was this her aunt's eczema, the mark of shame— when one is a woman, fat and vulgar, who works near the prison, for a swindler at Mazas? At last, having reached the limit of her energy, Catherine collapsed, Catherine capitulated: the woman who the evening before had felt a mysterious sweetness after having "killed" Leuven, but who now saw her hands covered with her aunt's eczema, dropped onto the padded seat of a large café, ordered a drink, and fainted on the table.

THE RIBBONS — END

Now she saw herself, lying down, in the guise of a very large creature.

At her feet and at her head, also of giant size, two men were busying themselves with her. One was none other than old Abbé Cary, but in the intervening time he had become a bishop. The other, a silver-haired old man with an intelligent, sardonic face, called himself "Professor Einstein." The holy prelate, the eminent professor, were in agreement in pointing their fingers at Catherine, both of them, in a profound commiseration. And each picking up a broad-bladed knife, they slowly carved out of this woman dark, spiraling ribbons about five centimeters wide and almost as thick.

XXIV

Avenues that opened and shut after so many excesses of grief, and after so much of what was allowed or was not allowed by the underground mind—one didn't yet dare speak; but since the majestic relaxation something had nevertheless happened, and she remained in this feeling of relaxation; to characterize her state of mind it would have been enough to use a single word: it was once again *possible*.

For instance, she knew that, in order to arrive, she had to conjure up the figure of the woman in black again. To conjure her up was mysterious and difficult. Once it was a sort of black doll thrown down into the stairwell, a doll which had to be picked up but which was extraordinarily heavy for a doll; another time, she herself was descending a broad stone staircase that led to the black water; in such water one could easily have drowned. On the last step, washed by the deep billow, something had to be discovered, for the deep, dangerous, very black water was also very *important*.

All the avenues interconnected and formed intersections. Parts of them returned insistently: for instance, the women in black. For instance, the women that had to be conjured up. One day it was she who had fallen, and a woman in black approached her, but she stood up herself in order not to be taken hold of. On the contrary, when the women in black were on the ground, the task was endless. How could one get them back up again, really?

Nevertheless, she did not doubt that she wanted to achieve something, and perhaps succeed in it at last. When she found herself faced with that mysterious black water, she certainly had to descend to it, and she experienced not so much fear as uncertainty and apprehension as to the motions to be made. If only she could go into it and come back out of it *before it was too late!* If only her problem with the black water could be resolved within a useful amount of time! If only—this is always what the man says—the catastrophe would not proceed faster than one's goodwill.

"What one kills at certain times one must bring back to life at other times," explained Little X. "If one has killed the dismal-fat-woman idea of our mother, and especially after having recalled the real fat woman who was the aunt, then the disgust has gone away; one doesn't have it anymore. So one must now find something else for this mother, and consequently for oneself: believe me, it's very important." But Catherine was losing her way in the painful labyrinth. And—it is hard to say this—she was not even so sure of the existence of Little X. anymore. This phenomenon that appeared in the evening, by moonlight, near half-open doors . . . Yet she loved it; and because of that love, the last that remained to her, Catherine did not want to know the truth, or free herself too much of the Little One. It would have required only a slight feeling of distrust to make the dear child vanish forever and ever. One word would have been enough, one unfortunate word. For the human tongue kills the rarest creatures. God, how dark the roads were! Little X. was arguing: "The ways out should be sought in what you have seen lately, when it indicates an *immense doubt,* an *insuperable difficulty,* and all sorts of things like that; look hard. The way of getting out of it is either to find the word that will make the coat fall off, or to raise up the woman in black who is lying on the ground as though after a crime." What a piercing intonation of the voice the Little One had for maintaining her absurd affirmations, and how useless it was to block one's ears!

One would have thought one was in a romantic dark valley where wounded horsemen were passing. The horseman on his horse, the woman near the horse, the horse itself—all were mortally wounded. Or—that year there was a lugubriously bright sun during the summer—one could see the horizons of the desert, whose sandy forms change so quickly but are always the same, where here and there sleep captive women who first have been raped, then massacred. For these women, it was too late.

XXV

COMEDY OF LOVE

Mademoiselle Noémi's theater had three sets, whose lighting one could vary: they were *the studio,* thus named because here one worked and typed; the modest bedroom, which contained a cheval glass; and a sort of nook used as a dressing room, which, except on occasion, remained dark. In each set scenes took place that could vary in one detail or another, but the play did not change—it was repeated regularly from its beginning to its end—nor did the actress—Mademoiselle Noémi—change, nor the audience—M. Trimegiste.

The scenes were without words. The slowness of their unfolding and their silence constituted their interest, in fact. The unfolding of the spectacle that Noémi had invented for M. Trimegiste's eyes assumed whatever rhythm one wished, for time did not count anymore; the scenes in each set and the three sets in succession slipped imperceptibly into one another; there was no need for a curtain. The place was: *a furnished apartment* of a young woman in Paris, in which the wallpaper is flowered but modern, the chair backs and mirrors oval, the cushions black, and where the flowers are always pretty white roses. The poetry of this theater was conventional. Isn't conventional poetry most suitable for enveloping a very secret action?

The meaning of the tableau was behind each of the figures, and its force depended on the *solidity of the emotion,* such as it emerged from the thing seen and thus passed like a block from artist to audience. It was therefore a uniquely lavish play, and in consequence of great depth.

M. Trimegiste, a businessman, is waiting for his secretary while smoking a fat cigar, and appears very flushed. The room is dimly lit and all the curtains are drawn. The scene brightens; the secretary in question is before M. Trimegiste, though no one has seen her enter. She is a very elegant young woman. The point of departure is open to many interpretations. One can't know ahead of time how the actress will continue. For instance, today she is wearing a mink coat and her head is encircled by a most distinguished Renaissance flounce; her stockings, her shoes are from the best manufacturer. She smiles distantly like a society person. Starting at this moment, M. Trimegiste falls into the stillest attention; the actress, in turn, adopts a "slow personality." She settles in, she sits down, she arranges herself on a silk couch; she tips her head back; she boldly, though slowly, throws one leg over the other, in such a way that the leg remains horizontal, suspended. Here are these brilliant, massive, complicated, quivering legs. The light fades. These magnified legs are in truth a team, like horses decorated with elastics and roses, which move along at the seaside, which is represented by the green and blue lining of the coat: they pull round masses and half-moons of an amazing weight and of a great softness, and at the spot where they join is a horrible secret, more perceptible or less, more distressing or less so, depending on the will of the draught animals and the importance of the trappings. The effects of these mysteries are infinite. Or everything can be as simple as ABC: the legs resemble commonplace snakes, and under the organdy panties, because they are transparent, appears the mound of Venus.

A poor student lives in a room with a cheval glass. Thinking she is alone in her own home one winter evening, she has made herself comfortable, unable to stop herself from questioning the sad enigmas of her life. She has loosened her clothing by unbuttoning all the buttons of her only buttoned dress from buttonholes that have been much used; she has removed a bra that was pink, and let her eighteen-franc ninety-five-centime socks slip down, until the moment when she must stop herself before uncovering her pudenda, which is strictly forbidden. Nevertheless, she unfastens the flap of her combinations. (One notices that her breasts are rather heavy, drooping, and her hips poorly shaped; this adds a good deal of charm.) The student as she lies there begins an anguished daydreaming. Tears in her eyes, she sees that the cheval glass is sending the image of her rear end back to her over her shoulder; or she thinks she sees it, for the relative positions prevent her from seeing the reflection but allow the framed reflection, in which "it" displays several dimples and seems sketched with a brush, to find the spectator, and it is the spectator who contemplates it.

The immobility that ensues, in the actress and in the audience, becomes dismayingly profound. They are no longer breathing. They are there. They daydream there. They abandon themselves there. One no longer distinguishes one from the other. The light dims.

One is now well along into the "petrifaction of the feelings." Everything is of stone: the bodies, time, the consciousnesses. If the first scene began at six in the evening in a joyful light, it is not surprising that we are still, at midnight, in a gloomy atmosphere in the tableau of the cheval glass. And if any energy remains, Noémi *drags herself* to the dark nook; it is one in the morning. What she does in the last tableau of her "mystery" is entirely conjectural, for everything is dark. But since one feels that she is there, one feels that she is almost completely inanimate, and that what she is doing, she does without a face. A sad human smell passes through the air from the rooms like an Oriental perfume.

* * *

The two of them were caught up together by an irresistible desire, and one signaled to the other. Or Trimegiste, arriving from his office, found Noémi putting on a ridiculous getup because she had had a "second sight" of her friend's desire. Noémi worked like a painter, with a skillful retouching, to change the signification of her canvas. And since not a muscle moved in these singular tableaux, they were soon forced to the idea that they were performing a ritual, a sort of holy thing, something much more than an ordinary exercise of love. How had they arrived at this majestic slowness, at this stupor in immodesty? They knew that its automatic and ritual nature, and its subtle mixture of relief and privation, necessarily lay behind their real pleasure and the moral justification (in the end) of their love act, that is, the reason for their love.

At last, it was over. They resumed their natural way of being, in normal light. Noémi had put on a dressing gown, carefully closed, and Trimegiste was trimming a new cigar. They talked about everything—the others, Catherine, business affairs, and future plans. If it wasn't too late at night, they ordered supper to be sent up from the restaurant on the boulevard. They contemplated marriage.

* * *

But who can ever say how our gentle sky changes into a hurricane? After the intrusion of Catherine, who had stuck her nose into her affairs, Noémi was provoked. No, she was not afraid of this large woman, this "washed-up woman," as they usually said. She, Noémi, had her whole life ahead of her! She had certainly let her know that, that washed-up woman. But all the same, Noémi was troubled. Inside herself she no longer felt as much like a statue, a figure on a stage. She no longer entered into her state in the same way. She was thinking about something. Since she no longer entered into that state in the same way, she no longer worked out the details. "No, I'm not afraid of that woman, no, I'm not afraid of that woman!" And Noémi began to tremble and to become terribly irritated. No—but it may happen that our enemy's eye reveals to us, better than any other, what we would like to hide from ourselves.

It is a very good thing to show one's rear end in a mirror, since it gives pleasure; it is a very good thing to *do what has to be done* with *the man one loves,* and so as to achieve pleasure, since that happens with him. But when Noémi showed herself, and when the man looked at her, then was the man's pleasure simply the reverse side of the pleasure she experienced? That would never be enough, never. Then would one say that the "theater" was not a love game? It was of supreme delicacy in the area of love because *it replaced love.* But why replace love? For the first time the question "what is love?" occurred to her with all it entailed. This subject of old reveries became at the present time a hard problem to solve. (1) When she put on her dressing gown, could she say she had been loved? She couldn't really. (2) Wasn't there something disquieting in Trimegiste's whole attitude? (3) Is or is not virginity the component part of marriage? Noémi did not waver on that point. Amuse oneself as best one can, all the while preserving one's virginity, which meant holding the future in reserve. (4) Aren't there all sorts of ways of leading a man to marriage? The principal method is still to please the man, and to give him proofs of submission in advance. (5) She would, of course, have preferred our parents' way, to receive a fiancé from her papa and be married in a white dress! But there were so many women better than she, and so many men who only wanted well-to-do girls! (6) One has one's own natural needs. (7) Impossible to displease Trimegiste. But now, after a certain time in which they had had this pleasure together, during which she had shown what she was able to do, why wasn't he coming forward?

It wasn't good on his part. It was bad. Noémi felt her talent was wasted and her faithfulness compromised. At the time of her apprenticeship at the Stenography and Typing School, she had heard those young ladies who passed around certain photos talk about seminal fluid, which they called "food." The word lodged itself in her head and came back to her insistently. Food! Food! Noémi remembered another man (Catherine's nasty friend) who had disturbed her a good deal, and she also remembered this: how he had disturbed her. Noémi recognized her desire, the only desire in her life, her heart's overwhelming desire: that by means of food she might have a child! A child of Noémi's flesh! What perfect joy in this world! How it was a growth that she had to obtain at any price! Food yielded a child, the child was food. All pleasures paled next to that one, which would issue from marriage; but wasn't having the child beforehand another procedure for precipitating marriage? Suddenly Noémi decided that she would obtain the child without waiting another day. And one would certainly see, after that! One would certainly see who was right, she or Catherine.

* * *

It was on a day of stormy heat that Noémi found herself thus taken captive and forced by her own will. In her usual getup, she was smoking her cigarette, mastering an intense fear. If she lost the match . . . she would also lose Trimegiste, but she would win the match. Yes, today—or never! She counted her heartbeats up to a hundred, up to five hundred, before interrupting their theater and walking up to Trimegiste! Noémi knew very well that she was running the greatest risk at the moment in which, the ritual interrupted, she would be nothing more than Noémi. If she passed the basic test that consisted in walking to him dressed only in her shirt, she was certain of victory. Alas, my God, how probable it was, how very probable, that she would be struck with paralysis!

Yet here she was close to him, in her theater disguise, but with a very simple manner; she had not done it on purpose and it was the moment when she was not believing in it at all anymore. Her downy eyelids opened and fell again over her eyes. Trimegiste must have been waiting for her, for he had stood up also, and Noémi saw with pleasure and hope the signs of his emotion. She had thought that a drama would explode as soon as she interrupted the theater; it wasn't happening. Here she was in his arms. Certainly Trimegiste would end with a "presto," that was her impression. The girl's breast was crushed against the gentleman's jacket.

Oh, surprise! The "presto" did not occur. M. Trimegiste appeared to be listening to the words of a very important voice, of a fatherly voice that was giving him advice, and what was that advice? It seemed that Trimegiste was perceiving, quite despite himself, a succession of serious facts which, in the midst of his overly impassioned feeling, he had neglected to consider and which were forcing themselves on him at this solemn moment. But the more hesitation she saw, the more Noémi, who did nothing by halves, concentrated on her idea, "I shall give myself," and the more Trimegiste, seeing this, listened to the fatherly voice. Thus, he kissed Noémi on the top of her forehead and on her eyes. "Are you weak?" said Noémi. Truly she lacked experience, and M. Trimegiste's goodness easily got the better of her. Panic-stricken, Noémi asked again, "Are you weak?" and did not try again; and was silent.

For the first time in his life, M. Trimegiste was cold; cold as a museum antique. Noémi played her last card. She cried to him in his ear, in the most vulgar, familiar sort of way, "Do you want to give me a child?" And she threw her shirt far away from her.

He shook his head, quite simply. Sweat softened his detachable collar, and he looked twenty years older. As for her, she sprang away to the back of the room.

Her eyes, Trimegiste noticed, protrude like those of a fly. "First of all, your head is too large. And then, you're depraved. I, give you a child—come now! You don't interest me at all." Noémi, who a moment before had been as pretty as a rose, had become as black as a spider. She changed again. She assumed a singular majesty, put her shirt back on, and said, formal again, lifting her eyes to heaven: "You're right. You are pure."

Then she studied Trimegiste, hatefully, preventing him by her violence from opening his mouth, and she pursued him with her look of hatred until she had made him leave the apartment.

(It was three days after this scene that Noémi Parchemin vanished, after having been seen for several hours in a Brussels hotel.)

XXVI

THE SIGNS

Two years!

Two years of this adventure, secret, spiritual, personal and not personal, what had happened to her and what had upset another's life—in which she had discovered through experience that "we are more bound to the invisible than to the visible" (Novalis). Two years which she certainly would not live through a second time; and this gave her the pained and silent face she had today. Two years during which there did not cease to appear, to recur, to exhaust itself by recurrence, always beginning again, the soul that had so martyred her in its lifetime, which we can call that Vagadu, that monster, with its dominance over the time when she was six years old. And now the autumn, which was the season of decline, seemed this time mysteriously pregnant with spring! Her strength, instead of diminishing after so much expenditure, increased, in the same way that the wood of the trees, scarcely stripped of leaves, seemed to her to be making young shoots, new leaves again, all over.

So what did this white hair matter? What did this hand matter, thin as it had become, with rings that floated around her fingers? What does a diminished body matter, or age or poverty, when we are approaching the movement that contains our salvation? "Ah," said a man in a similar situation, "ah, the last turns of the wheel . . . " During long hours, one meditates on a bench on a boulevard in an unfamiliar neighborhood. In the armchair of a picture gallery one remains deeply surprised, and one loses the notion of time and of one's space. One does not exhaust the subject matter of reflection. To think about oneself is no longer egotistic, it is thinking to achieve the highest form, the idea of oneself. For years, one is searching for *one's own* expression; one wants to write *one's own* poem. There is no daydream in this: nothing but work on facts. For years, perhaps for centuries. Because of the greatness of the work undertaken, the importance of the salvation, one tolerates everything: failures, dialectical difficulties, losses of energy—when, after having clarified a point, one falls back onto another point in the confusion—in short, the sort of bewilderment in which one lives. One tolerates even misfortune, which no longer spares you and strikes on the outside those to whom you were attached, which strikes them and strikes you indirectly; through their fault, through your fault, or without its being possible to distinguish a determining fault; the moment when one lifts oneself up again is that of the most tragic coincidences. It seems that everything is being given the cue to fall. But one wants to write *one's own* poem and there is almost nothing left that one can tolerate.

For Catherine, it was a matter not only of shifting masses but of attaining conversion. It was necessary to attain belief, to believe in oneself and in own's own life and, higher than one's life, in "the vision of something which is beyond." How very dull and immobile love still was, even separated from its dark roots, more or less well washed! How absent were tenderness, adoration! She felt, then, not in control of her movements, but conveyed by them toward the positive, toward the negative, so opposed to what the reality of the moment would have desired that she be, a sky so dazzling on one side, a storm so lasting on the other, that all she could do was persist.

Her new state had been preceded by these signs.

                              * * *

In the courtyard of an aged house, where the old oil painting is covered with a coating of grime and spiderwebs (in fact, it was the rue Jacob, the house she had lived in for ten years and where she had known her greatest happiness), she saw the carriage entrance and, beneath the overhang, as is customary, the bin for the household refuse. This occurred on a beautiful summer evening.

Rarely, the last cars went by. Yet Catherine was going out; she was going to spend the night with a stranger who had been giving her the eye during the day. Catherine wanted to hail a car, but they were horse-drawn vehicles, or they were very old automobiles, and all were occupied. Catherine's cheeks were hot because she was going to this rendezvous, but she had stopped short: a woman was waiting for her near the bin.

This woman, with a light face, had smooth hair; but most importantly, her hair was blond. She had no personal expression; in her bearing and the form of her clothing she manifested humility. Was she a penitent? One might have thought so. What was she doing waiting in a neighborhood like that, all too similar, herself, to the distress of the long summer evening? Catherine stopped close to her. Catherine spoke gently to her, which the person was probably expecting, for she rose up, she came out of her immobility close to the metal container, she rose up, like a plume of smoke.

She displayed a singular decisiveness in passing through the courtyard window to enter Catherine's apartment.

Now, inside Catherine's bedroom there were three very white beds. The first, the second, the third—these were certainly the beds of the three sisters, of Catherine and her two sisters; and Catherine, being the second, occupied the second bed. But the woman, with her rapid step, headed toward the second bed; she went up to it, she parted the sheets, she lay down in the child's bed, with a smile of unspeakable happiness. She was putting herself inside Catherine and she still had her pale face of a short time ago, next to the refuse, but since she had come out of the refuse, her pallor had changed meaning, left shame behind to arrive at joy.

HE SPREADS THE LIVING BREATH

And this was the second sign.

There was a garden, of very brown earth; this garden lay on a table, at the height of a child's hand. Thus the child could put its hand into the pathways and onto the trees. And the mother (the blond one) was showing the little girl that one should take the flowers with their fat, white bulbs, bury them in the earth, and that they would grow. The little girl was next to the mother; from her height she looked at everything the mother was pointing out, the garden table, the flowers, and finally she followed with her eyes the figure of the mother in everything the mother was doing, in everything the mother was. (It was certainly the same woman who had withdrawn from the garbage the evening before.)

The child, learning the natural history lesson, wanted to make the flowers grow. She looked for the white bulb, which one was supposed to bury in the earth. Ah—but the flowers—they had been cut! The flowers she had been given were cut and had no bulbs. Since their bulbs were cut, they would never grow, never more in the earth.

The child, in despair at that, saw the three beds reappear on the garden wall. An old song could also be heard, with a foolish refrain such as "Nevermore, nevermore" in English, and which concerned quite particularly the second bed. The child therefore went over to the second bed; she was going to put flowers on it, at the head. Since this was how it was, the flowers were for the second bed.

She opened the tall window that was behind the bed.

It was night. Close to the forest. Night, but no longer completely night: before dawn. Almost dawn. And the forest, the beautiful forest, back after a long time in which it had been forgotten, was black, soon green, in an endless thickness, but one could say this time that it sparkled with blackness. The sparkling black forest and the sky trembling toward gray corresponded strangely well, and everything, at the same time, seemed to have been cast together, the sky and the earth, like gold.

From the forest came the Man. Admirably distinguished, he had bare shoulders, and lower down wore some insignificant clothes. In his behavior and his laughter he was fifteen years old. In his strength in general he was a man and had had children himself. His tenderness was that of a five-year-old, no more. Oh, what a surprising hero! On his head, a gay paper hat.

Then the Man, who as he passed was singing a noble mountain song, noticed at her window little Catherine, the admiring little girl. And he came very close, very close, and he came close enough, breaking off his song, to *blow,* as he passed, on the child's head.

He had passed and she was still looking, she was hoping to see him again . . . But now she also saw a great fire on the left, and in this blaze he had disappeared. But the little girl felt her heart had become larger than the forest and the world . . . for the breath, a marvelous breath, was still touching her on the forehead. She was very, very happy. Never again would she lose this happiness. She had been baptized. She had . . .

XXVII

WRESTLING WITH THE ANGEL

. . . The intruder appeared in the shadow and struck her first on the thigh. It was as though she were expecting it; for without jumping at the pain she thought only of gathering her arms and legs, hardening them, putting her body in a posture of resistance. And the tears that came to her eyes did not spring forth; there wasn't time to cry. She felt a second blow, in the groin. Blows received in the groin make a woman cry out. She cried out. She asked where he was, in the pitch dark. Her hands, flying out around her, touched him, caught him. She sank her nails into him with a force that astonished him. He moaned. He was therefore vulnerable. They would soon be equally matched!

They panted together, watching for a chance to strike.

Leaving the middle of the room, where she had been when he had attacked her, she leaped against the wall, and it was here that she was chest to chest with a stranger who had said, "You will die like a dog."

"Oh, I haven't been able to live!" grumbled Catherine. "Oh, I won't be able to die . . . You'll see!"

Her own plan was to tear out his eyes, to blind him. She had formidable nails. His plan was to break the woman's back, but he was also angry at her private parts, so he hesitated and lost ground. She, on the other hand, did not hesitate. Her hands were sticky with his blood. Under the pressure of a pain too intense, one or the other would howl in turn. Yet the strength they had at their disposal grew greater and greater, and it was clear that their strength was identical. In this gloomy darkness, in which objects were shattering around them, would they arrive at a decision? This was why they stopped using surprise attacks and crudely nasty methods like those they had been using. Standing against each other and partially nude, since shreds of their clothing, clawed to pieces, were falling off, they fought economically, soberly, without shouts or tears. The point was still to bring death to the enemy, but by the long path of exhaustion. Catherine felt within her incredible reserves full of energy, which she had never before in her life had to experience, and which had accumulated for the purpose of this hour; as for him, he was strength itself, which restores itself as soon as it is expended. Catherine was quite likely to receive death, after a proud combat. She also hoped to achieve victory. While they wrapped around each other and rolled on the ground, their skins covered with bruises and wounds, she tried to find out who he was: "Who are you?" But she would have to kill him before she could unmask him. For an infinite length of time they remained thus blocked and confined by their rage for destruction; they reduced the struggle to movements that only kept it going, for they knew that victory would belong to the one who could breathe the longest. He who had attacked, she who was defending herself, were giving up on murder, and soon they would give up on hatred, even though the fight was more necessary than ever. She saw a strange pleasure erupt within the horrors of the struggle, which had nothing human about it. Then she heard his voice: "You are the saddest of creatures, now. Consent to die."

"I should kill myself like the other one? Me? No."

"One person is worth another. One woman is worth one woman."

She wanted to strike a blow at him that would once again be atrocious in order to reanimate their anger and hasten the outcome. But as she applied herself to pinching him and twisting him in a certain way, she felt that perhaps from this moment on he would cease to be vulnerable—without threatening her anymore, as long as she kept on defending herself like a lioness. It was that one could see, through the cracks, the grayness of the dawn. The light was going to appear and the adversaries would be able to recognize each other.

He said to her: "I have not been able to overcome you. Let me go."

She answered: "Not before I have had your pardon."

"Do you think you will ever manage to get free of your fault? In your fault you developed and you acquired the strength of your arms."

She answered, still fighting: "I'm not afraid of your reasons either. I have struggled with you. I will struggle with you."

He said: "Sin has need of law, law has need of sin. Sin and law are one and the same."

"I would certainly have liked to destroy you," said Catherine, "but I also love you. Who are you?"

"Why ask me my name?"

Then she was sure of an extraordinary change. She still pressed down on him, like a victor, but it was with the feeling of obeying him. She was fighting so that, as she took on the appearance of the one defeated, she might receive life from him. She owed him everything. All of a sudden she didn't understand anything anymore. She wiped off her body, which was bleeding and covered with sweat. He had opened the door, he had vanished. She collapsed onto the floor.

XXVIII

The Paris light appeared harsh and gray behind the blinds. She awoke in the middle of the morning on her couch to the sounds of fresh music. She stood up, with great difficulty, for her body was broken by blows. She looked at her room, where shattered objects lay on the floor. She went out on the balcony; she shivered with cold and pleasure, before the beauty of the spectacle. The bitter, dirty space laden with factory smoke was as beautiful as the azure above Solomon's temple. "Come back, come back, Shulamite . . . " The music continued to develop and begin again exultantly; for all of this was: herself. In the midst of the musical fog she thought she saw two horses with white breasts standing on the roofs, looking at her with their women's eyes.

She became afraid of her joy. She went back in.

She did not know how to use this certainty she had. She wanted ardently to put it to the test. A sudden wind blew her hair up over her face, coming from behind her, in the hallway, as she went to Flore's room. As soon as she saw Flore through the half-open door, she went back the way she had come. Flore was looking into the courtyard; she "knew" what had happened because she seemed happy at last—the way she had been long ago, in the time of Catherine's youth, when they had first met.

Catherine saw Luc Pascal at three o'clock in the café in a very majestic avenue under the sparkling light and the grace of a noble winter's day. He was expecting to find her different, and not so gay, luminous, and without makeup, with a sort of strength in her body; they hadn't seen each other since . . . no point in saying what event.

* * *

"I scarcely recognize you," M. Pascal remarked right away, looking at her first in full face, then in profile, then reflected in the café mirror. Catherine did not like such affectation.

"And I, too, scarcely recognize you," confessed Catherine, "but I don't like your insistence very much."

They were silent.

"I have the impression"—he was still trying to find out the reason for her disorder—"that something isn't there anymore."

"What sort of thing?"

"A certain quality, I should say a certain shame, lovely and heart-rending, which used to be in the depths and up to the edge. It isn't there anymore."

"Is that thing necessary to you?" she said, laughing.

"Indispensable."

"In that case, we've taken our positions!"

He backed down and said, "Not at all, I'm waiting for you, and I hope I will understand."

"Understanding won't give you the thing."

He said enigmatically, "I don't know anything about it."

She spoke out right away, because this was a game that couldn't really be played together: "My friend, we have been lovers for a year and for six months now we haven't seen each other. Furthermore, I have almost finished a serious revolution. I think I have enough strength and warmth for a new experience between us; I also think I am amenable enough to end the experience here. As you like."

The tone of this speech was extremely displeasing to M. Pascal, who couldn't tolerate such great freedom coming from a woman. He scowled.

"A love, Catherine, can't be treated like a take-it-or-leave-it matter."

"I agree with you," she said.

Yet an idea was fluttering about in her heart: I will ask the question; he will answer and I will obey.

"Talk to me about yourself," said Pascal in a softer tone.

Catherine made her eyes dart from right to left and from left to right, without answering.

"How do you explain the disappearance of the character I talked about?"

"How worthy of pity," said Catherine, "how lovable, was Fidelio's prisoner. But if he comes into the light . . . how antipathetic is his thinness and how unlikely his position: he must be thrust back in prison!"

This time she laughed openly.

"No, Catherine," said Luc Pascal with great earnestness, "God is my witness that I was never one of your jailers."

"Do you believe that, Luc?" she replied, still gay.

Luc Pascal sensed, to an intolerable degree, Catherine's *tranquillity.* His mood was dark.

"It's not possible for anyone to change you! Your name is Crachat, that's a predestined name. You were 'born,' as they say, in society. An orphan, sickly and poor, you drifted in the gutter of Paris. You shone there, with a false sheen. You are the woman of the greatest quality I have ever seen; you are worth a million times more than your acts; a sort of modern angel, you contain an infinite mystery that refers to nothing. That is your nature. For the love of God! Let all this remain in a good way."

"That was a pretty portrait," said Catherine. "I don't know how to tell you, it seems *old* to me."

"Could you be the victim of a conjurer who surrounds you with incongruous objects, changes the shape of your nose, and causes a reasonable person to rise up out of you? I don't acknowledge that he has any power to touch the real Catherine."

"The late real Catherine," said Catherine. "It is painful to see your intelligence so miss the mark; and anyway, this discussion is distancing us from the two of us."

"My intelligence," retorted Luc Pascal, "is prepared to admit everything that has a basis in the truth, even if it be the most distressing to reason and the most scandalous to humanity."

"Then," said Catherine, "say what I am."

"Illusion!"

"You see that your intelligence is not prepared to accept . . . I won't repeat the phrase."

"Well, that's probably so," said Pascal, more quietly. "And if that were the case, I *don't want* it to be."

"Good," said Catherine sadly. "Now we're back down on the ground, you and I."

"Don't think we're so down to earth. I say one doesn't change!" said Luc Pascal, as he walked along the boulevard, for they had left the café. "One mustn't change! It's only a question of burning everything in a certain manner, and I had hoped that you would bring new materials for a more intense fire. Quite the opposite of what happened. One mustn't rest at ease on any point at all of one's fate. A high sort of life is often the complete exploitation of an infirmity. Every life is tragic. One must say, like the other: I will come, and in order to come I would come on my knees, and if my legs were cut off I would come on my belly!"

"That's just what I'm doing," said Catherine.

"A moment ago you talked about Fidelio's prisoner. That prisoner who must be *put back into prison* could perhaps represent you; but I'm the one he represents, certainly. I have always needed to be in prison. I admit there's something unhealthy about it: I don't care. I'll be able to accept it. I'll live on the left side and give up the right. I tell you: quite the opposite of what you're doing. The characteristic of the *true* prisoner is that he returns spontaneously to his prison. You were forced to be a prisoner; I'm a voluntary prisoner, and I will even say an ideal one."

Luc Pascal was now talking to himself, as though in a dream. "Love is worth nothing to me. Love spoils what it touches (acts of love, I mean). Certain people have a very unhappy way of loving and it would be better if they abstained from it. God created me for solitude and the twisted life lived 'aside.' I probably intruded violently into your destiny—as I had done to another woman before you—and the only way I will console myself for that is by thinking that I was the instrument you needed (which very fortunately I did not understand). Let us separate, Catherine. And you who appear to be 'new' and who are no longer very attached to this artifice of love that we have made together, leave me to what is my role without feeling even a shadow of remorse. Doesn't each person play *his own* game? I'm leaving like a thief, extracting a secret from you that I will be able to use!"

"What secret?" said Catherine. "You are hurting me, Luc."

"Then don't be hurt. I don't know anything about the secret. It's primarily a secret for me. But it comes from you. I will remain your oddly faithful friend."

As he was about to say good-bye to her, he seemed to change his mind. "I have to tell you something else that's surprising but good for you in the end. I have news of Noémi."

"I beg your pardon?" cried Catherine.

"Noémi, that's right. She's alive. She didn't kill herself in Brussels the way everyone thought. Now she is teaching school in a city in Morocco. She has resigned herself to her fate and is satisfying the demands of her job. She doesn't have a pleasant memory of anyone."

"Oh, good," said Catherine, "she's alive."

She did not try to find out more about it.

And now, little by little, they had arrived at the spot where they had first met, when they had left the costume ball together. Pascal noticed it first and remarked that that was nice, and Catherine, infected by this feeling, also recognized the spot. They hesitated, then after exchanging the same look they embraced, like two travelers; they remained in their embrace for some time. Catherine moved away. "Good-bye, Luc, good luck," she said.

"Good-bye, Catherine," Luc answered.

Both added at the same time, "See you soon."

He went off toward the south, she toward the north.

XXIX

Catherine was free and alone for the first time. The direct and surprising feeling she had was that within her there was an ascending power, but that she had to use that ascending power to create her freedom each day. This was how she first experienced it.

THE PUMA

She has the power to sit down at the table, which is old, heavy, and round. She has the power to open a thick book that lies on the table, and she can read this book. She is alone. She is in good health.

She reads secret things, very profound things, which explain themselves. The large cat comes of his own accord and leaps onto the table. He is very handsome; this is her cat. He has sparkling, sleepy eyes, pink lips. His name is Poom! His eyes are green. How he leaps, see! How he leaps and how he rolls, this brown and black cat, over the table and over the book, playing with all this, displaying his pretty fur; it doesn't bother her in the least.

She takes hold of the cat's head, she strokes it.

Immediately he grows larger. He grows visibly larger and around him the space multiplies rapidly. It's a path along some high, arid plateaus, which are themselves at the summits of mountains. It's a forest that has only one giant tree, and immense jagged rocks, small because of the distance. On top of this Tibet there is nothing human left; one has no means of preserving oneself. The cat, the beast, occupies the center, the middle of the solitude. He is as long as a man at present, and as powerful as ten men together. With his neck planted with spots and tawny, and his chest with its silvery hair, he could frighten Catherine with his military air, if she did not know that once upon a time he was her cat and that she has maintained an understanding with him. He flails the sand with his magnificent tail. He fills the landscape more and more, but will he even stop at the landscape? He is also in the water of this bathtub of rocks. He is also on the clouds that sleep on the backs of the eternal snows. He does not stop growing. His bloodshot eyes displaying the highest degree of femininity, he rolls, he abandons himself in the things of his superior universe. With the claws of his many paws he does not stop taking and touching bodies, and swimming in the bathtub, and running over the rocks, working matter and light in a thousand happy ways, in order to destroy them and shape them and remake them, the puma of this abstract land! And what a puma! Fortunate that Catherine once had rights over him when he was her simple cat. Otherwise she would be eaten! No one will ever think of hunting this one! He does not stop playing and romping under the clouds, threatening the whole world, and loving, with his powerful thigh, and also eating what he loves, and straining and relaxing his body on the high ground!

In the end there is nothing but him, red, and the sun. His womanly eyes are volcanoes. His hairy tail is the Milky Way. His maw opens like a trumpet . . .

* * *

What tenderness and what confidence one felt when, after having for so long doubted his reality, one knew that the Beast was there. How can one help feeling that it is he who gives the atmosphere its color, and the limbs their pleasant suppleness, and the intelligence its elasticity, and thought its clear-sightedness and its hope! The Beast was a beautiful beast. It alone truly opposes that cold administrator of justice, death. Yes, the judiciary seems to be winning out in the last place, but is this so certain? For in the Beast, through its profound, its distant consequences, life overflows the human person and . . . Now the Beast was free; at the same time it was judged. Knowledge of the thing with its trait of truth also shows us its limit, and where its power weakens, and where the other thing will begin.

XXX

On the promenade that ran alongside the river, Catherine heard behind her the little step she knew so well. She allowed herself to be followed, very happy, slowing her pace. She got onto a tramway and felt that the other was getting on too. And as soon as she was in her room she saw the child. The Little One sat down in her garnet armchair as usual, lit by her own light, and arranged in a suitable way her old-fashioned dress with its big bow at the back. The Little One was more peculiar than she had been before, and frankly conspicuous, like a fantasy through which one could have put one's hand and at which one would soon have to smile. But her face, her sweet face, was so familiar to Catherine that her trust returned.

"Oh, hello, you!" said Catherine.

"Hello," said the Little One, smiling in a friendly way.

In truth, Catherine was already talking to herself, and she became aware of it. Did the Little One have enough dominance to borrow Catherine's voice? Or was it the opposite, that her reality having become "apparent," she was no longer so implacable, and in this case it was Catherine who was taking over the Little One. But Catherine's emotion was stronger than her need to analyze, and she said to her, "I'm not thinking of myself, I'm thinking of you and I love you." The Little One seemed enchanted with a painful modesty.

"You have seen how our affairs have gone. I was always waiting for you; I said to myself, 'She's going to come back.' Then, I confess, I forgot you. It was because I was happy. Forgive me. You know, it's so good to 'say yes,' for I 'say yes' now."

When Catherine wanted to express her gratitude to the Little One for the inestimable help she had given in the most difficult moments, the Little One shied away from the honor and even the affection, and shook her head.

"Oh," said Catherine, "why don't you allow me the happiness of thanking you?"

Then Little X. began a curious evolution. She changed form rapidly, feature by feature, face by face. Thus her body became twice as long; it was covered by a black lace dress with a train. In her face, more or less the same, her eyes assumed a remarkable melancholy intensity. Over the lace appeared an apron, and over the young girl a chambermaid; the blouse had filled out; the face, unrelated to the preceding one, had acquired beauty. Finally, a further thickening: a woman, this time, was dressed in a silver material twinkling and puffing out like a modern crinoline; inside it she breathed with emotion, her thin arms resting on her haunches and an artificial rose encumbering her shoulder; casting a guttersnipe's glance to one side, she breathed, as she strutted along, because her partner (invisible, outside the frame) was going up before her.

"Stop!" said Catherine. "I recognize you very clearly. All these figures that are passing represent my failures. Tell me how I am to reconcile myself to so many failures? How am I to reconcile myself, really, to you, Little One, to whom all this has happened? It's certainly you, swarthy girl, prematurely buried because you had guilty feelings, and for a long time you tried to avenge yourself. It's certainly you, it's certainly me; but the guilty feelings are no longer guilty—so will we be able to reconcile ourselves? You're not speaking at all anymore. You are a mute shadow. But you're not going to leave me this way, for I no longer want to be unhappy. All these failures of our life were forced to occur because it was you, always you, who ran out from the background and began crying out again, always the same cry—always the same cry, because I didn't want to hear it and no one else suspected it existed. Thus all of that was forced; all of that was obligatory. All of that added together the way two and two are four; and that's how it is, because it is so inevitable that one can find the way to reconcile oneself with you. I don't bear you a grudge anymore for these misfortunes; I don't bear a grudge against myself anymore. If one shows a human soul a little crack toward light, toward freedom—oh, how strong and joyous it feels!"

But in the manner of *Little snail on your bed of slime—please to tell me the time,* the forms folded back into each other and everything came back, in a turning motion, to the point of childhood.

Little X. reappeared in her garnet armchair, smiling with her four-penny face. Vaguely close to her, putting his hand on her head, Louis Moutier. A little behind, the Father, absorbed, smoking a cigarette, while from afar and almost with her back turned, the blond mother looked at the Little One with indulgence and irony. These four dead people were motionless, but no feeling of sadness issued from them.

"Good-bye, now, Little One, you can leave me," said Catherine, sighing. And she explained: "You will be able to leave me. As you see, things are ending well."

The Little One had tears in her eyes and on her cheeks; they looked like tears of glass.

"Dear, poor, only friend," Catherine went on, "what will become of you? You won't have anyone now."

The Little One opened her eyes wide, like someone who is being murdered.

"No," said Catherine, "not that way. That isn't good. Not that way."

The truth was that the Little One still had a certain thing on her mind and wanted to ask a question, one last question. As for the meaning of the question, Catherine made it out without too much difficulty.

It was: "Was my face really so black? Was I so nasty? You said I was swarthy."

Catherine stared at the Little One, closing her lips and ever deepening the loving look she gave her. The Little One continued, tearfully, "Tell me something?"

Catherine, with the tips of her fingers, blew her a kiss.

Then the Little One smiled, and truly vanished.